THE SOUND OF DISTANT THUNDER . . .

It was a booming, eerie, low-pitched sound of violence. It came toward them with the speed of a rocket, and even as it did, Don was moving, seizing Zees' arm, dragging her toward the boat.

The earth leaped under their feet as they started to run toward safety; they staggered as if drunk, and they could see the force of the quake moving toward them in the form of a distinct wave in the trees. Trees were falling everywhere, their crashing adding to the roar of approaching thunder.

Then it was upon them and they could not stand. The jungle floor heaved, and the world came crashing down upon them. Then there was only a deadly silence. . . .

Thunderworld

by Zach Hughes

A SIGNET BOOK
NEW AMERICAN LIBRARY
TIMES MIRROR

Publisher's Note

This novel is a work of fiction. Names, characters, places, and incidents are either the product of the author's imagination or are used fictitiously, and any resemblance to actual persons, living or dead, events, or locales is entirely coincidental.

Copyright © 1981 by Hugh Zachary

All rights reserved

SIGNET TRADEMARK REG. U.S. PAT. OFF. AND FOREIGN COUNTRIES
REGISTERED TRADEMARK—MARCA REGISTRADA
HECHO EN CHICAGO, U.S.A.

SIGNET, SIGNET CLASSICS, MENTOR, PLUME, MERIDIAN AND
NAL BOOKS are published by The New American Library, Inc.,
1633 Broadway, New York, New York 10019

First Printing, January, 1982

1 2 3 4 5 6 7 8 9

PRINTED IN THE UNITED STATES OF AMERICA

Deem not life a thing of consequence. For look at the yawning void of the future, and at that other limitless space, the past.

—MARCUS AURELIUS

Thunderworld

BOOK ONE

The Explorers

ROAG the Rememberer, who was first eaten in the Season of the Red Comet, said this:

Love him, the eater of your lost youth; praise him throughout the act of knowing the World.

Thus it was that Roag the Rememberer came to be denied the honor of ultimate fulfillment, was lost in the darkness of melt, was denied the joy of blending and the healing trauma of the teeth of the eater. When life was new, to love the eater was not in the nature of the people.

Roag, melted, lived on, for he had invented history, and that concept lived on after him in the minds of the assigned Rememberers. Roag alive angered Moulan the Strong with his concept of love. It was then that Moulan, inventor of fire, developer of order, first of all the people to discover fulfillment, also invented fear and death.

1

GOROIN Melt of Roag hefted a stone atop the barrier which was slowly closing off the narrow entrance to the canyon. He accomplished the task with a grunt and then sat back on his long-muscled haunches to pant wearily. He was old. He was tired. He rested. But from inside the narrow canyon, from the waterhole which formed below a stream bleeding out of the high scarp, he heard the hissing roar of the Great One. The sound moved him, his emotions soaring, giving new strength to the feeble limbs. He worked with his heart pounding, his forelimbs hanging tiredly as he made his way to the rock debris collected at the base of the scarp.

His hinged legs were designed for leaping and running, not for moving heavy burdens. His forelimbs held but a fraction of the strength of his long legs. The fingers of his forelimbs were agile but weak. He was severely limited in his ability to move the fractured and jagged stones. He selected small ones. He had been working a long time. The barrier was growing. He could allow himself a precious moment. He stood, his ovate body trembling, to peer down the dry canyon. He saw nothing, but he could hear the splashings of the Great One as the beast celebrated the end of weeks of desert browsing without liquids in the coolness of the clear mountain pool.

He measured the barrier with his eyes, panted to gain quick strength, and continued his work. As the light of the sun dimmed, his pace was slower and slower, his burdens smaller and smaller. In the growing darkness he was topping the barrier with stones no larger than his small doubled fists.

He knew that the Great One would sleep near the water, perhaps in it, his body submerged to give him rest from carrying his own huge bulk. Goroin would sleep near the barrier. In preparation, he loosed the string of his pack and pulled forth the light skins which would be both bed and cover. He spread the sleepskins and fell onto them, his overburdened heart slowing at last, even as his spent limbs jerked in painful protest. His eyes lidded swiftly.

He awoke in total darkness to the pains of the world. The earth beneath him lifted, jerked, fell, heaved, and there was the thunder of it in the distance, low and long. He judged the severity of the earthpain to be minor and dismissed it with a sigh of thanks. It would have been unjust if, after his long, lonely seasons of search, after his incredible luck in finding a Great One, his hopes had been shattered by huge masses of rock rumbling down from the jagged scarp to cover the rare Great One under crushing mass.

When he awoke again, it was a shrouded morning. Fine ash coated the sleepskins. A small cloud of dust rose as he stretched one long leg after the other and threw the skins aside. He stood, inhaled, primed his sneezing mechanism and made a snouted grimace as the accumulated dust was expelled from his nares.

The sky was low, a roiling, rolling, dark gray, a thing of apparent solidity, his sky, the sky of his world. From far away, from the direction of the land of eternal fire, he heard the low rumble of atmospheric thunder, but he knew that the rain clouds would be deflected from the desert by the towering, icy mountains beyond the scarp. For this he was thankful, for he would not be faced with an onslaught of abrasive, muddy rainfall as he waited.

He folded his sleepskins carefully and placed them inside the hide pack. When the pack was safely stowed in a crevice at one end of his barrier he tried to move his limbs and found them to be sore, weak, aching.

He froze in midmovement as he heard lumbering footsteps from within the canyon. Then there came the braying, harsh, hissing call of the Great One. His long ears stood, and he felt a growl grow in his throat. He dropped into the shelter of the barrier. It was not yet time to be seen.

The footsteps came closer. He reacted to them with tremors of excitement. He could smell the great beast, could feel its presence. And then he could look up and see the long, slender neck extended over the barrier. The great reptilian head swayed. Dull eyes saw the sky and the canyon beyond the barrier, but not Goroin, below the extended head.

Gorion knew fear, not of the Great One, but for the integrity of his barrier. The piled stones came only to the knees of the Great One.

"Oh, World," he prayed. "Oh, World."

The Great One did not try to climb the barrier, nor to merely step over it, nor did he try to push it away with his great bulk. Inside that admirable head was a brain large in size, minuscule in intelligence. The sheer bulk of the beast ensured implantation into that brain of an instinctive fear of loose footing. Any fall, for that mass of flesh, could be disaster.

The Great One voiced his frustration in a fearful bellow. The very hairs inside Goroin's ears seemed to vibrate with the roar, and he was left breathless in admiration.

"Bellow, Great One," he said silently, as the angry, puzzled roar was repeated. "Bellow, my Great One, but you *are* Goroin Melt of Roag."

The thought sent his mind whirling in expectaton of newness and fulfillment. During the days of waiting which were to follow, his need would become a breast-filling ache.

On the morning of the second day following the completion of the barrier and the Great One's first attempt to pass it, the fall of ash had lessened, there having been no major thunder of earthfires during the night. Goroin awoke to great body pain. The excitement of the search and the ecstasy of discovery were abating, and the toll of his efforts was being felt by his aging bones. When he moved his legs he could hear creaking sounds. He could hear his own groans.

He arose to check the barrier. It was unchanged. Nevertheless, he policed it from one end to the other, moved a small rock here and there. The effort made him vomit. His upper stomach had long been empty, so the heaving produced only a bitter bile. When the heaving stopped he crawled painfully to his pack. The left rear leg of a springer, taken days previously, was dry, tough, slightly rank, but it was food.

He leaned his furred back against the barrier, held the leg and chewed long and thoughtfully. It could be the last food his body would have. He felt quick concern. Without conscious order his force searched out, darting and swooping to cover the area which stretched away from the scarp. There was only lifelessness.

He told himself that the food would be sufficient. He forced himself to be calm and, as a sop to his worry, peered over the barrier. Visibility was good, but the Great One was hidden, near the pool, by an outcrop of rock.

The sounds which came to his ears were reassuring. The Great One was growing restless. Goroin heard tough hide scrape on rock and imagined that the beast was searching for another way out, picking his way carefully among the fallen boulders on the canyon's floor. But there was no other way out. The World had provided. The only spring of clear water within days of walking was at the rear of a narrow, high-walled canyon with only one outlet, and the barrier blocked that.

Almost as if it were an omen the midday clouds swirled high and there was a clear area over the near desert. The blessed sun shone through, poured down through the clearing to make light. Goroin moved to enjoy the rare moment, lifting his snout to feel the sun's energy on his face, to let it soak in, to feel it prickling deep down inside. He reveled in the sun and in the sudden drop in temperature. For long, delicious moments he was, at heart, a springer again, but soon his body sagged in tiredness and he limped back to the barrier to wrap himself in his sleepskins against the chill. Idly, he watched the lights and shadows play over the barren landscape, and he practiced the art of Roag, that which was within him, and he was young and there had been a clearing of the sky and he was romping in the sun and suddenly, wonderfully, *she* was there. She was even younger, still training. And was new and discovering and was to be named. She was Melin, once Melin the Fruitful, lately eaten, to be named by him, to be called, in closeness, Melin of Grace.

World, how he missed her. How it pained his heart to miss her, the warmness of her, the glad joy of being two together, the sunny, exultant discovery of the fullness of life there as they danced and capered in the sun and chased and fell and rolled together panting. Ah, how young she had been. How they looked into each other's eyes when they felt it rush over them, the knowledge that they would blend.

To leave her was not injustice, not true sadness, for she was younger and his time had come and there is an order in the world which cannot be denied. One ages. One is eaten. One begins anew. That something, or someone, is left behind is the order of things, for Melin, too, would age, and be in pain, and she would seek the eater. The world provided. If the world willed, they would be together again.

But where was Melin's Great One?

His Great One approached the barrier on the third day, bellowing in frustration. His Great One pushed against the barrier with one knee, gingerly, fearfully, lest the rocks fall and become unsteady under the great, splayed feet. So fearful, so huge, and so invincible, once life gave intelligence to that brain. Thank the World that the beast was so stupid, so fearful, that he did not realize he could breech the puny barrier with one push of his extending chest

Goroin had fed on the last of the springer. He sang happiness, but silently. It was not yet time. Good omens persisted. His body rallied. He no longer ached. There was in him only a knowledge of diminished power, a reluctance to move. The sun shone, a fiery roundness, through a clearing of the yellow-gray sky. And that night, as he heard the Great One moaning in hunger, as he knew the time was near when the beast's instinctive caution would fall victim to the tyranny of the need to supply food-fuel to that great body, he saw the white lights of the night sky, watched them for a long, long, awe-inspiring time before the roiling ash clouds closed them off.

But before the clouds made total darkness he saw still another omen. There, in the midst of the thickest lights, against the black which was as silken as the new fur of a dark springer, he saw it, the omen, his own omen, for one of the

sky lights moved, slowly, but it moved as surely as he was
Goroin Melt of Roag, as surely as he knew the history of the
people through Roag's gift. And in all the history of the
people, in all the brief and inspiring observations of the lights
in the sky, none had ever moved.

2

A WATER world announces itself to instruments from a million miles away. Captain Donald Duckworth knew this to be a fact, for the ship's instruments had been tested thoroughly using his own planet, good old blue Earth, as a target. Had the instruments not been tested to detect Earth's generous supply of water he might have doubted the readings which began to appear when the starship *Santa Maria* blinked out of subspace near a feeble, yellowish, Sol-type star.

She was a sick-looking little star as stars go, smaller even than old Sol, and her signatures showed that she was young. She had no name, not then. She'd been analyzed from sixteen light-years away while the *Santa Maria*'s huge generators built power for a jump. A.J. Agagin hadn't even wanted to check her out. A.J. tended to go for the biggies, the impressive giants. They had almost missed her. Over two years in space, over four hundred light-years from home, and they'd almost missed a water world, had almost used a big blue giant as a blink beacon to start the wide circling movement back toward home. Over two years and that incredible distance and uncountable jumps powered by old Jonathan Blink's miracle down in the hull of the big ship and instrument analysis of a thousand planets and they'd almost missed the only one in over two years.

Ellen Partance, on instrumentation, looked at him and winked one big blue eye. "Since A.J. discovered her, we'll call her Agagin's World," she said.

"Unless there's a very small one on the other side of the sun she's a three planet," A.J. said, ignoring Ellen's teasing.

9

Hell, a man can't be right all the time. The little yellow star hadn't looked too promising. The biggies tended to be the most likely planet producers. Most of the smaller ones just swam alone in the endless night of space spurting out their energy into nothingness.

"A three planet," Ellen said. "Like home."

"That remains to be seen," Duckworth said. He was a large man, but trim. He kept himself tan under the ship's lamps, was a fanatic for physical conditioning. His hair was bushy, brown, and in need of a trim, but he wasn't thinking about having Zees give him a haircut. There was a water world out there.

"Shall I call Zees?" Ellen asked. "I don't think she'd want to miss this."

"Sure," Duckworth said. "A.J., figure us a near miss and let's take a look."

Agagin was already figuring. His dark fingers flew. He had the blink coordinates before the fourth crew member of the *Santa Maria* came rushing into control, her light-brown hair mussed from sleep. She was buttoning her blouse. So all four were there to share the moment when the generators hummed and there was that peculiar little feeling of being displaced which ended almost as quickly as it had begun and four heads looked automatically toward the port, which was closed, and then to the viewer.

"Oh, no," Zees breathed, as the viewer zoomed in and saw thick, roiling dust clouds.

Agagin and the captain were going through a checklist. Duckworth's voice was crisp, unaccented. Agagin spoke more softly. The gyros began to wind down from their high-pitched hum. There was a lessening of static tensions in the air as the generators came to rest.

"We're tucked in nicely," Agagin said. "Want the orbital figures?"

"Long as you're sure," Don Duckworth said. In two years and five months he'd learned that he could rely on any information which Breed Agagin gave him.

"Let's take a real look," Ellen Partance said. She was a tall woman, hips flaring slightly in the comfort of a shipboard tightsuit, hair tucked, red and full, under a nonregulation hat.

Ellen was that sort of woman. She always had to do some little something to show that she was not merely a cog in the wheels of the Space Service. Duckworth, in command, understood.

Zees pushed buttons. The radiation shield over the viewport hummed into the hull. The view was impressive, as always when looking down on a new planet, but disappointing. Instruments still insisted that there was a considerable amount of water down there, but the atmosphere was a boiling cloud of dust.

"Got anything, Breed?" Duckworth asked.

"Very interesting," Agagin said. "She reads good. Along with that dust, lots of silicones, there's some pretty decent air. And she still reads one helluva lot of water."

"I make it volcanic dust," Ellen said.

"Well, it makes sense," Zees said. "She's a chick of a young sun." Zees was the youngest member of the crew. She kept her hair cut short to sweep forward onto her cheeks in an antique style which accentuated her large, almost oriental eyes.

"Maybe it's smog," Don said, with a wide grin. "And when we go down we'll find a pre-atomic culture down there making steel and filling the air with combustion products."

"Volcanic ash," Ellen said.

"Probably swamps," Breed Agagin said. No one called him A.J. Half Choctaw, half white, he was the Breed, the Halfbreed, named early in the trip by Ellen after they'd viewed an antique movie from the ship's library of microreels. The usually staid Agagin rather liked it. He had been the studious type, the type of boy who is never given a nickname. He'd had to grow to be seventy years old, halfway through his allotted span, and travel quite a distance before someone liked him well enough to give him a nickname, a love name in Ellen's case.

"Life?" Duckworth asked. He'd put the ship there. Now it was up to him. He wasn't helpless on the instruments, but he wasn't as fast and efficient as those who had been trained to use them.

"No big concentrations," Zees said, after some study.

"Not much of a sun," Ellen said. "If it weren't for the

cloud layer I'd say the average temperature planetside would be just below freezing."

"Not much of a planet, either," Agagin said. "About three-quarters Earth size."

"Well, she's the only planet we have at the moment," Duckworth said.

"Whoops," Ellen said.

"What, what?" Duckworth said. He was an anti-whoops man, hated surprises. One bad surprise aboard a starship can be the last surprise. They were a long way from home.

"Earthquake," Ellen said. "Big one."

"Lots of volcanism," Zees said. "Pretty impressive stuff."

"Don," Agagin said, "get me those readings we made of the sun."

"Next week we've got to get organized," Don said, after an unsuccessful search. He aimed outboard meters and began to take information from the local star. He had his readouts just as Ellen found the previous readout, made from a few light-years away in the direction of 32 Vulpeculae and Deneb and Earth.

"We were a bit off," Zees said, studying both sets of readings. "I'd say all we have to do is wait about two billion years and we'll have a Sol-type sun."

"The first billion will be the hardest," Ellen said.

Duckworth groaned.

"The volcanic ash must be giving a greenhouse effect," Breed said. "Otherwise there wouldn't be any free water to read, only ice."

"Swamps," Zees said.

"Steam," Ellen said.

"A Precambrian world," Breed agreed. "Maybe some bugs, primitive life, nothing really interesting."

"Don't knock that," Duckworth said. "We're not looking for intelligent life." They were looking for living room. They were looking for a lifezone planet, a water planet, and the more they looked the more evident it became that old Earth was one of the blessed spots of the universe, the rare one, the one which had formed directly in the right spot, at just the right distance from just the right size of star to have water exist and, thus, to form life.

"Who's going down?" Ellen asked.

"Not you," Duckworth said. "I won't risk losing my doctor." They'd been through it all before, at each planetfall, each time something down there on some godforsaken ball of rock warranted investigation. There had been many planets. There had been Mars types and Mercury types and a couple of Venus types so shrouded with poisons that no deep exploration needed to be made. But this was the first water world. This one might, just might, be usable. This one might take a few of the crowded billions off the groaning crust of old Earth and give them a place for new hope and relieve the home planet, slowly, of the killing burden of overpopulation.

"You and Zees went last time," Ellen said.

"Ellen, when you learn to make a portable generator recite the multiplication table like Breed and Zees, you can come along on initial exploration. Until then, forget it," Don said.

"Actually, he wants my strength," said Breed, "in case of alien monsters."

Duckworth was tired. His arms felt heavy. He stood and stretched. "Your watch, isn't it, Zees?" Zees nodded. "I suggest that you two turn our new mudball over to the automatic monitors and follow my example, which is to get some sleep."

Alone on the bridge, Zees made her routine checks. Around her the *Santa Maria* hummed and clicked. She was a good ship, crowning achievement of Earth technology. And she was one of only three. The *Nina*, the *Pinta*, the *Santa Maria*. Quaint. Going way, way back for hope, for the names of the ships of a displaced Italian who set the scene for some very nasty competition between two halves of a world when he sailed his ancient water vessels into the unknown.

Four hundred light-years. But their trip, even though so much more impressive in sheer distances, had been made in more comfort than poor Columbus enjoyed. There were private quarters and a gym, library and film room, a lab and a mini-observatory.

The ship was both the pride and the hope of the western half of her world, and as such she bore a great responsibility. She'd been built, along with her sister ships, over great objections, both at home and abroad. People were going hungry on old Earth, and there were many who begrudged the time and materials and wealth spent on space. The big resentment had begun, Zees knew, at the time of the Great Expedition. There had been an uneasy peace, an era of cooperation, and the whole world had participated in building the fleet which, using the old, inefficient, barely predictable nuclear engines, had blasted away from Moon Base to disappear.

Zees had not been born when the great exploration fleet left Earth to find new planets, new relief valves for the exploding populations. Don Duckworth was just a boy. But Zees had heard recordings of the primitive radio communications with the fleet as the distances grew more and more vast and it took years for the signals to reach Earth. Men still listened, monitoring the assigned channels, hoping against hope, but the cynics said that the Great Expedition had been the Great Folly. They cited the good which could have been done on Earth with the outlay of wealth and talent it took to put the fleet into space. They gave up hope. And it was differences about the fleet which set the stage for new disputes between east and west.

It was hard to believe that in the modern world, with Jonathan Blink's new theories making it possible to cover in moments more distance than the fleet could cover in years, men could still hate, and dispute the few things left on depleted Earth worth disputing. It was hard to believe that after the total nuclear disarmament after the turn of the century, nations were once again building the bloated, deadly bombs.

There were times when she almost felt guilty. She was, in a way, a symbol of the new tensions, for it was a Texan who, in his own private laboratory, much to the consternation of the governments and corporations who spent billions on research, had developed the first really practical sublight drive. And the west's reluctance to share the discovery had become a critical issue.

Earth's troubles were far away, but they were there as Zees stood her watch, as the automatic monitors gathered information about the cloud-covered water planet below the orbiting *Santa Maria*. She hummed quietly. The others slept. Around the ship the seven planets of the little yellow star, sharing perhaps a dozen smaller satellites, marched through their orderly routine toward the eons which would see the little star mature. There was an asteroid belt between the fourth and fifth planets, and a wandering comet was just discernible on the ship's instruments.

She opened the viewport and looked down on the roiling atmosphere of the small water world. She felt like weeping. There had to be livable planets. Now that Earth had the means to move people—the power of the blink drive was relatively unlimited—there simply had to be planets of water and air and growing green things. Otherwise there was no hope. Otherwise the family squabble over food and land and the diminishing resources of Earth would grow and—

About that, she would not think. As it had been to millions before her who had faced the same threat, *that* was unthinkable.

3

DON Duckworth was awakened by a sting on his arm. He opened his eyes in time to see Ellen swab the spot. He himself rubbed the hickey which blew up where Ellen had injected nutrient spray. She knew he hated the thing and when she could, she shot it into him as he slept. That spray, which did something to slow the little biological clock in his system which said age, age, was one reason why, unlike his ancestors, he was not an old man at seventy.

"I put in a few extras," Ellen said. "Build up your antibodies in case there are bad bugs down there."

"Gee, I love that medical talk," Don said, rising to pull on his tights. Ellen took no notice. Ship's crews were not chosen on the basis of sex, but after two plus years aboard a ship as small as the *Maria*, modesty took a beating. Moreover, the crew of the *Maria* had proved to be very compatible. It was not the first time Ellen Partance had seen the ship's commanding officer in the nude.

Zees was seated in the command chair, feet up on a console. She was humming when Duckworth entered. Seeing him, she smiled. "I'm not sure, but there seems to be a faint life reading down there now and then."

"Sabertooth tigers?" he asked.

"Even if it's a young planet it can't be all bad," Zees said.

"Is Breed awake?"

"I wish you'd take me," Zees said.

"It's Breed's turn," he told her. "Did you by any chance send our position?"

"No," she said. "I was going to wait. No need raising

16

hope back home until we find out for sure what's down there."

Behind them, stretching backward toward Earth, each segment straight, a zigzag line marked by small blink beacons was their link. In theory, it was possible to blink from one side of the galaxy to the other. In practice the stars and space debris got in the way. A ship which blinked too close to the gravitational well of a star would, although it hadn't happened, most probably be destroyed or, at best, tossed to the far reaches of the universe, never to find its way home. Blink travel was, by necessity, slow and painstaking, and each leap taken by the *Maria* had to be calculated carefully, aimed by the shipboard telescopes and instruments to go only so far as a straight line extended without approaching mass. A message, on the other hand, could travel home almost instantaneously, being relayed by the preset blink beacons. With blink coordinates established, a ship wishing to travel the same route which had been traveled by the *Maria* on the way out could make the trip in a fraction of the time. There were, however, no other blink ships, except the two sister ships, and they were off in other parts of the near galaxy doing the same thing *Maria* was doing, looking for a lifezone planet.

"There's an interesting weather system down there," Zees said. "There's a hurricane blowing in the southern hemisphere. Mountains along the equator keep most of the weather in the south. It's rather strange."

He studied pictures. She superimposed a grid and indicated the probable landing area of the ship's boat. "There's an area of calm here," she said. "The jet streams run up high and move the dust clouds and make it look rough, but on the surface it's strangely quiet."

"Almost unnatural," Don said.

"That's not a wild statement. Look." She pointed. Instruments had been constructing a computerized profile of the landmasses of the planet. "Look at these mountains. It's much too much. They are extensive and huge. She's probably as unstable as hell."

Duckworth ran a hand over his face. "Well, we'll do a thorough survey from the boat."

"At any rate, this looks like the best landing spot," Zees

said. She put her hand on his arm. "I don't have to remind you to be careful, do I?"

He grinned.

She went back to the growing computer image of the landmasses. "Isn't it strange that she's a three planet, just like Earth? We've talked lifezone all our lives, and I never knew what it meant, really. The ratio of her size and distance from her sun is the same as Earth's. And just the one water planet. The others are little balls of rock or gas giants."

"I guess systems are all formed the same way," Don said.

"If so, why haven't we found an Earth in each system?" she asked.

He shrugged. "Punishment for our sins?"

"It makes one wonder. The conditions for formation of a lifezone planet are so elusive. Sometimes it makes me wonder if Earth isn't unique after all, and if we weren't put there for the sole purpose of peopling the galaxy."

"We were put there to fornicate," Don said, "and overpopulate."

"Exactly. To fornicate and make things so miserable on Earth that we're forced to go out and people the galaxy. So why aren't there more habitable worlds?"

"Maybe we were supposed to stop breeding after a while."

"Or learn to live without air, or in subzero ice, or in boiling ammonia."

"Easier to stop fornicating," Don said, grinning.

"Hmmm," she said.

"Or be sensible about it," he amended. Her lips were heavy. In two plus years they'd come to know each other well. "Stop it, I'm going planetside."

"Breed isn't ready," she whispered, lowering her feet from the console and coming into his arms.

Thus occupied, they missed seeing the brief clearing of the skies over the desert. Ellen caught it on film a few minutes later.

"We'll go down here," Duckworth said. "We'll land on the flats near the high scarp."

"Sixty-two thousand feet of mountain up there," Breed said, pointing.

"Hidden under permanent smog," Ellen said. "A shame."

"I've been doing some calculations and I was right," Zees said. "She's a little unstable. She wobbles. The mountains throw her out of kilter."

"Gee, I love that scientific talk," Don said.

"I can see the ads now," Ellen said. "Live a life of high adventure. Experience ash storms and earthquakes and volcanic eruptions. Risk the ultimate thrill of a planet shifting on its axis."

"We'll need a good name," Breed said. "How about Agagin's World?"

"Precipitous," Ellen said, "for the mountains."

"She's not going to tip while we're down there, is she, Zees?" Breed asked.

"I don't think so. She's not wobbling much. She's a lady who hasn't made up her mind, though. She's still forming mountains. That biggest landmass is too much in itself. I suspect continental breakup is just beginning. She's quite hot on the inside, and that heat might help the greenhouse effect to keep her unfrozen. Volcanism can release a terrific amount of heat. There are probably a dozen major quakes a day. There's one huge amount of strain on the crust. And when I say earthquakes, I'm not talking about a Southern California tremor. I mean like tossing up the Rockies."

"I think Ellen said she wanted to go down with you," Breed said, making as if to remove his pressure suit.

"Knock it off and let's go take a look," Don said.

4

TWICE before the unseen sun sank to leave the world in cooling darkness, the Great One made futile excursions to the barrier. Each time Goroin studied him and admired him. For perhaps the first time in his life he could understand what old Roag had meant, for it was difficult not to love that great head, that long and graceful neck. His awe and admiration were, indeed, akin to love, but perhaps that grew from his need, from his awareness that his body was growing weaker.

He used the time for inventory and remembrance. It would be important to have all his knowledge refreshed, so that it might resist the trauma. So it was that he lay alongside the barrier and let his mind journey backward in time, to reexperience his long and peaceful life as a free one in the desert with the delightful Melin of Grace, to remember his last flowing and the pain and to know that it would come again. And beyond that, into those areas of his mind which were different, for he was Melt of Roag, and although that which had once been Roag was no more, there were the pockets of information which had been gathered by Roag the Rememberer and emblazoned into that life stuff which had melted. He knew that he was unique. He had known no other Melt, although there were others.

The time clung, cloyed, crawled. The night saw heat, trapped beneath the roiling clouds, close down over the desert, and it was comfortable to lie uncovered. The morning brought no change in weather, but as Goroin tried to arise he was astounded by his new weakness, and the food was gone. Oh, World, had he waited too long?

Then the dull eyes of the great beast were peering once more over his barrier, and the Great One was making a low and desperate noise of hunger deep in his long neck. Black, moist nostrils twitched as the beast smelled the freshness of the sparse desert growth and longed to be free, to roam the flats and search out the tidbits of vegetation. He was a creature of the desert, the Great One, and his powerful legs would carry his bulk many marches in a day while the long neck lowered to browse the scant vegetation or to dart out and seize an unwary food creature.

"Soon, Great One," Goroin said silently. "Soon it will be over and we will stoke the furnaces of that huge body with good flesh." He could almost feel the beast's panic, the yearning to move, to be freed of the blockading barrier. And he knew that the situation was becoming quite delicate, and that he would have to choose his moment carefully. If he waited too long the fear of death by starvation would overcome the instinctive and powerful fear of loose footing and uneven places. If he showed himself too soon the built-in caution of the Great One would foil everything, for in a time when all of the free-roving Great Ones had been taken, all save, perhaps, the Great One of Goroin, the beast could not have survived without knowledge that the glow of life in the eyes of his prey dictated flight, not attack.

When the Great One went back to the water to try to kill hunger with great gulps, Goroin sank within himself, slowed the painful beating of his tired heart, began, once more, to review his inventory of memories and knowledge. Twice and then once more he was able to start with newness, through the memories of Roag the Melted, and to see the sights gathered by Roag and remember the newness, the almost total learning process, of Goroin the New. The number of seasons had no meaning to him, but they stretched back and back.

Such self-examination produced some new thoughts. The people looked upon a melt as weak, a being of marred unity. He could, while knowing the world through two sets of memories, his own vivid ones and the scarcely known ones of the melted one, come to the conclusion that he was not marred. Indeed, if anything, he was somewhat blessed. He had never been handicapped by the presence of a subset of memories, for he dominated them, used them only when he needed them. For example, although he had never left the high desert he knew the land of the fires. He knew the heat and the feel and the smell and the dangers as great earthpains racked the land to the south. He knew the dangers of the trek and the cold of the high passageways between the towering mountains. He knew the feeling of inadequate air at the mountain heights, and could remember how young lungs had pumped the harder. He could feel the cold and the unbearable tiredness.

What he did not know was Roag's reasons for the trek. Knowledge? Of what benefit was it to know that the land of fires was a deadly place where one risked the flow of fire and burning mud and the fall of so deadly a curtain of ash that not even the strongest could lift himself from the crushing burden? Yet, one had to admire the Historian, for he had the ability to understand. If one knew, for example, exactly what Roag had meant in his talk of the love for the eater, if one could understand and not become confused by the word, itself, into comparing Roag's concept with male-female joy, then it all might come clear. What was love? Was it his feeling when he entered a fruitful area of desert on a clear, cold day and discovered the young Melin, unnamed, newly eaten, her new body uncoordinated and waiting to be trained? Ah, but she was a joy, reverting in her enthusiasm to the atavistic two-legged hop, rolling in playful awkwardness as they blended, soft-furred, fully rounded as the new body was altered by life and began its rapid growth into maturity.

"One does not hop," he had told her laughingly. "Hopping is the mode of movement for springers. One, how do I explain? One falls forward, vaults, in a way, from one extremity to the other. The weight of the body falls forward and is caught, halted in its fall, by the placement of the other leg."

It was a characteristic of the people. It separated them from the springers, that mode of bipedal locomotion, but to a newly young Melin such concerns had no importance and she tweaked him and hopped away. In love, he hopped after her, for he was not long past having been eaten, his body vigorous, agile, capable of limitless travel in the high desert. It was a harmless exuberance to hop like a springer, to feel the powerful legs thrust together and send the body soaring to leave the earth for a joyful moment.

"That is better, glum one," Melin of Grace called to him, as she hopped, leaped, felt the air brush past her face, seemed to merely brush the earth as she sped ahead of him. She made daring leaps across earthpain crevices, skipped from boulder to boulder with a laugh and gay invitation to follow, if he dared.

True, he had, in his long life, blended with other females, but it had never been as it was with Melin of Grace, not even in the shadowy dimness of the memory of Roag, whose female accompanied him to the land of the fires and was fearful.

Once, in a serious moment, he had asked Melin, "Can it be weakness to know the experiences of another?"

"I care not for heavy thoughts," she had said.

"But do you care if there is the shadow of another in me?" he'd asked.

"You are Goroin," she had said simply.

And in his age, in a body which had to be urged, tended, lest it cease too quickly, before the Great One had been rendered sufficiently ravenous, he could live it all again and wonder. Roag, too, had once been strong and young and able to capture the most elusive springer as it hopped-darted among the rocks. And then Moulan the Strong invented death.

If life itself was a mystery, then death was an enigma. Perhaps others had known death, before Roag.

He had time. He could not, however, answer the unanswerable. He came to a concentration of his fading energies; the effort to keep the failing body alive was becoming almost more than he could handle. But there was a part of his mind which was detached and remembering. Melin, he remembered, could not imagine living with a shadowy self, however dominated, and she gave up trying with a tweak of his snout and a laugh.

"Life is unending," Roag the Historian had said, and he had been, in that one respect, wrong, for Roag lived no more. Life can be destroyed. Animation is not life. Life requires animation, however. But the active springer was not life, nor was the Great One, impressive as he was. Animation was, in general, for eating. Animation was for bountiful food and how wonderful was the world, to demand, through love and blending, a constant replenishment of the springer bank. How wonderful that the hunger of the people was not ravenous enough to threaten to reduce the springer population.

Was he, Goroin Melt of Roag, on the verge of a new thing, a new thought? Not even Roag had dwelt on the difference between life and animation.

He could not get it right, and he gave off the effort and floated free. He considered the eater and the eaten. There were tales—he himself had never seen such a horror—of life eating life. The result was madness. Two life units in one body was, in his mind, the ultimate terror. Roag the Historian had seen. Long, long ago, Roag's memories told him, there had been such a horror. It was in the form of a great beast, one of the long-dead ones whose bones could be found now and again when digging near a sunken water source, a four-legged animal of fur and great claws and teeth, and from its eyes there had come a madness which, even remembered, caused shudders. It was a thing of total evil, two life units fighting and the great four-legged beast trying to run in two directions, unable to cope, starving, bones protruding through the fur.

Perhaps it was his state of mind, the knowledge of the end of his body influencing his normally sunny thoughts, but he dwelt on it and delved deep and saw the blasted forest still smoldering from a rain of fire and the animal in the distance, a rather magnificent animal, half the size of a Great One. He had seen a free one once, and had followed, enraptured by the grace, the ability to cover great distance in a bound, the power of the muscled shoulders and legs, the smoothness of movement. He had followed and hoped and in the end, although he presented himself and closed his eyes to hide the glow of life, the animal had, with a howl of fear, bounded away. And now there was another, gaunt, moving jerkily, falling to writhe in uncontrolled spasms. He approached. He saw the horror shining from the red, scared eyes. He used the limits of his young body, hopping like a springer, to escape that terrible struggle of two life units bound, the madness beating at his own mind, sapping his strength. To be sucked into that fetid morass of insanity gave wings to his limbs. And yet he could not leave the thing behind. He was bound. He was of the people. He gathered his courage and, luring the starving animal to follow, ran to a narrowing crevice where the great claws could not reach.

He blinded the great, maddened beast with a torch of fire and stayed in the crevice, his own stomachs growing empty, while the weakened, blinded, insane thing howled and tried to reach the flesh sensed by its scorched nose, until starvation weakened the beast and it was possible to free the trapped life with one mighty blow of a huge stone held over his head and thrown downward with all his strength. Two precious life units, melted, were free to float and search and find.

In the dark, dim areas of memory he saw Moulan the Strong, and he could believe the whispered tales that Moulan was the melt of such an unnatural union. Having once been mad, bound to another life, he, although melted and renewed, had dark sides to his character. Yes, it made sense.

Life is long, eternal. Life is precious. Not even melting, although it is death, is extermination, for the life goes on with a new personality.

Long, long ago Roag the Historian had said: "We must exterminate the predators. We must, forever, end the danger of double occupancy."

And, "Ah," said Goroin Melt of Roag, as he remembered. Was it there that the hate of the eater originated, in the youth of the world? Were the bodies and the brains of the great predators independent enough to dominate life and thus to allow the terror of double occupancy? Was this why Moulan reacted so strongly, long after the predators were exterminated, to Roag's advice to love the eater?

He himself had seen Moulan. He was a magnificent one, a Great One. He had seen Moulan from a distance, for his was not the temperament to submit himself to Moulan's Rules of Order. Moulan was large and grand and beautiful from a distance, a true King of the Great Ones. And he had known, in the shadowy memories of Roag, the power of Moulan, had felt himself being crushed under those hard, horny, clawed feet. He had felt his life screaming out without flow and then the blankness of floating, the loss of self.

It was frightening to Goroin to feel the blackness so strongly. He'd never felt it so strongly before. Perhaps it was because he'd made his mind receptive as he waited, as his body became weaker. The people had called it shame, to know the memories of a melted one, but it was not shame. He was interested. He tried to delve deeper, but it was not to be. His mind began to wander and to know fear, for the death pains of his body were strong, the overburdened heart was failing. For a panicked moment he considered trying the flow before the naturally cautious beast was sufficiently starved.

The Great One came to the barrier again, and he hoped, examining the large eyes carefully. There was still a glow of awareness. But it was slowly being replaced with the feeding frenzy. Soon. Soon.

There were alternatives. Perhaps he could summon enough strength to leave the barrier, find one of the lowly food animals, return in that form to tempt the Great One at the proper time. But the risk was too great. He might fail to find a food creature and the body would die there on the desert and he would float, melt, to, oh, World, become aware of three sets of self? Could one survive such? He would not try.

"Hunger, Great One," he whispered, as the beast went, once more, toward the water. "Grow restless and ravenous and be blind to the light of life."

Oh, World, he hurt. His mind wandered. He went back once again to the joy of Melin of Grace and wandered the desert with her.

"Melin," he said aloud, "you are there. You are there somewhere in the desert. I will seek you, and find you, and I will be fulfilled and then, together, we will search. Perhaps he is not the last Great One, after all, and then, with you fulfilled, we will live and own the vast desert."

But first there would be the long-awaited meeting with Moulan the Strong, for if Moulan was King of the Great Ones, this Great One which would be Goroin Melt of Roag was King of the World.

Muddy rain came during the night. Water collected. He drank for the first time in days and felt revived. The Great

One, his eyes showing more and more of the feeding frenzy, tried once more to find a way past the barrier. He bellowed, and the sound was the agony of hunger, the desperate need to stoke the fires of the huge furnace which was his body.

Soon. Soon.

5

THE boat's instruments, after two circumnavigations of the planet at the equator, proved Zees' suspicion to be correct. The planet was unstable. She spun on her axis at roughly Earth rate, her days being only minutes shorter than an Earth day. But because of the mountains and the large northern landmass she was wobbling, the force of her spin tending to try to balance the unequal crust load. She was slightly pear-shaped. A ring of fire circled the south. The southern ocean was aboil with old, new, and forming volcanoes.

Human eyes were useless in the thick atmosphere. Don Duckworth, flying the ship's boat, relied on his instruments as, the preliminary orbits inside the atmosphere accomplished, he lowered toward the northern desert.

The survey made by the boat had completed the computer picture of the planet.

"Volcanic ash makes good soil," Breed said, trying to find something good to say about the planet.

"It has to cool, first," Don said. His attention was on his instruments. He went in slowly. He saw the flats of the desert from a mere five hundred feet and selected his landing place carefully. An earth tremor shook the boat as it touched down, and he sucked in his breath and lifted swiftly, putting distance between the boat's hull and the heaving earth. When the quake had passed the boat landed without event.

"Aside from sulfur and other unpleasantness the air is pretty good," Breed said, checking monitors. "It's rich in oxygen, richer than Earth. Carbon dioxide is pretty high, not too bad. Nitrogen a little below Earth normal. Nitrous oxide higher but acceptable.''

''Atmospheric pressure?'' Don asked, as he went through his checklist to leave the boat's generator on hold, ready for instant liftoff.

''A fraction higher than Earth,'' Breed said.

''Bacteria and virus airborne?''

''Negative.''

There were some questionable spores in the air. They'd have to be checked out before anyone tried to breathe the air of the planet.

No good purpose was served when they left the boat, but it is the nature of man to want to set foot on new places, not merely observe them from the safety of the boat. Duckworth went first, turned to help Breed down from the hatch. They stood on sand. Barren rock showed through. Here and there were greenish spots of sparse vegetation. Visibility was roughly a hundred yards. Nothing moved in their field of vision.

''I claim thee in the name of man,'' Breed said, raising his armored arm and extending his hand as if in blessing, ''and I christen thee Absolutely Worthless.''

''Let's make a short walking survey,'' Duckworth said.

''Roger,'' Breed said.

''Gee, I love that kind of talk,'' Don said, striding off. They walked a tight circle, not losing sight of the boat, although their in-suit instruments could have guided them back to it in total blackness.

They had covered about a hundred feet when a tremor shook the ground and caused Don to lose his feet. He sprawled and dug his gloved hands into the undulating ground. The tremor rolled past to be followed by another, and then Breed was lying on his stomach beside him, saying, over the communication channel, ''Hey, now.''

They saw the animal together. They saw it while the second shock was rolling and the sound of it was that of distant thunder. It was a cross between a frog and a kangaroo in appearance, about as large as an Earthside pussycat.

''It likes the quake,'' Don said, as the little animal leaped and cavorted, using the rolling shock to spring into the air.

''Damned thing looks as if it's laughing,'' Breed said.

The shock ended. The animal disappeared quickly, hopping away from them.

"It seemed to time its upward leaps to use the heaving of the ground as a springboard," Don said, still amazed.

"I'm scared out of my socks and it's enjoying itself," Breed said.

"Let's get some samples and go home," Don said.

"I'd like for Ellen to take a look at that little animal," Breed said, as they walked quickly back to the boat.

"There'll be time for that later," Don said. "First we've got to determine if there are any baddies in the air or the soil."

Back aboard ship they turned their samples over to Zees. She disappeared into the lab.

"It's Worthless," Breed told Ellen.

"No diamonds lying on the surface?" Ellen asked.

"We didn't even get indication of heavy metals," Breed said, "but that's just on the surface."

Breed went to the bar and came back with bottles and equipment. "There are many reasons for drinking," he said. "You drink because you're happy or because you're sad and want to be happy. You drink when you're down because you want to be up and you drink when you're up because you feel so good and you drink when you're disappointed."

He drank. Ellen joined him and then Don, after Zees had made a preliminary report that there didn't seem to be any really mean microorganisms in the samples, joined both of them. Zees, her work finished, made it unanimous.

"I am going to become very, very drunk," Breed said.

"Why not?" Zees asked, lifting her glass.

Why not, indeed? They were four hundred light-years from home with the hopes of a world riding with them, and checks of too many solar systems had found only gas giants and rock balls, and now that they'd found a water planet, with the trip more than half over, the boat's instruments had recorded four earthquakes in one hour and that was in the stable area, on the high desert.

Why not? Back on Earth, people were starving and the pressures built and the politicians had failed once again and hate was abroad as it had been for the better portion of human history. Why the hell not? Zees made the stuff herself, in her own little lab, and she was good at it and could make it taste like bourbon or scotch or gin. The only trouble was that her hangover remedy was not nearly as effective as her booze.

Don was headachy and bilious. He had no desire to go back to Worthless. They were due a day of rest. They used it and others in small blinks to examine the other planets in the Worthless system. Near the weak sun was a sun-seared ball of rock hot on the sun side and cold on the outside. The two planet was Venuslike, with a thick, swirling and highly toxic chemical atmosphere. Four was arid rock. Five was a gas giant with a couple of iced moons. Six was a blockbuster, a Jovian planet on a titanic scale. She shot charged particles at them from fourteen million miles away.

"She's probably got a low-class nuke furnace in her gut," Zees said.

"Love that scientific talk," Ellen said, beating Don to it.

Six's magnetosphere reached sunward for over seven million miles. She showed heat, more than she received from the sun. She was the nearest Jovian miss ever to be discovered, but the *Maria* was not on a mission to collect pure scientific data to amaze the Earth.

"If she had gathered just about fifty percent more mass during formation she'd have been a sun," Zees said. "Then that little planet back there would be quite nice."

"After her inner fire cooled a bit," Don said.

"Yes," Zees admitted. "In fact, with the greenhouse effect, with Six a weak sun she'd be too hot for life."

"And when her fires cool and the volcanism stops and the dust settles she'll be too cold," Ellen said. "I think we should move on."

"I want some more of this one," Zees said. So the *Maria* sneaked closer, as close as she could and still weather the storm of radiation. The inertial field of the blink generator made it possible, deflecting the hard particles.

She was a mother of planets, in the form of moons. She was a failed sun, and she filled three-quarters of the sky with a dark and brooding and monstrous mass. On the nightside Six showed a fringe of yellowish brown. Around her bulk the stars were dim pinpoints. A moon swam into nightside and

they watched in respectful awe as space was lighted momentarily by a titanic bolt of static lightning flashing out from Six
to strike the moon.

"We don't want any of that," Don said.

"Give me one more minute," Zees said.

He gave her a minute and blinked the hell out of there.
They took a brief look at an ice ball, the seventh planet.
Breed discovered that some radiation had leaked through the
inertial field of the generator and clouded one of the cham-
bers. It was not serious, but a clouded chamber cut down on
the efficiency of the generators. It would take two or three
days to clear the damage. The place to do the job was in orbit
around Worthless. So, since they could not go on, a more
thorough survey would be done while Breed worked on the
generator.

On the way back Ellen found gold and, suited, went out to
chip a large nugget from a space rock floating in the asteroid
belt between four and five planets. She said she was going to
have a ring made of it. Zees wanted a nugget, too, but Don
said no. He parked the ship in a stable, close-in orbit around
Worthless and while Breed went to work on the generator
made plans to map and explore the planet. Ellen complained
when he told her she'd be holding ship while he and Zees went
below. But the only medical doctor aboard was too valuable to
risk. Without her knowledge, without her mixture of nutrients
sprayed into each crewman's arm about twice a week, things
would go wrong quickly. That little biological clock inside
each human which told the cells to age would start ticking
and make up for having been put on hold for seventy years,
in Don's case, and there would be almost instant aging.

Ellen, therefore, would help Breed with the generator, if
needed, keep shop, receive data from the boat.

For a thorough survey, the logical starting place was at the
planet's north pole. The boat hovered there, made instrument
readings. Then it began a slow but thorough circling of the
globe. There was ice at the pole, but it ended quickly as the
survey began to cover the northern landmass. There was
vegetation in the intervening tundra.

It was slow and boring work. The boat seemed to be
motionless in a windstorm of moving clouds, the clouds thick

with dust. They saw nothing, the instruments doing the seeing. The boat was small, but not uncomfortable. The couch, designed for one, was large enough for two, and once again Don marveled at the computers and psychologists who had so successfully chosen four people from hundreds of applicants with such success that after over two years in a closed environment there were very, very few instances of static among the four, no petty jealousies, no irritating clashes of personality.

Sometimes he had to laugh inwardly when he realized just how compatible the four were, and two together, he was sometimes awed by the closeness he had developed with Zees.

With the boat on automatic, imprisoned in its tiny cabin, they were content and complete and there was still a newness to their togetherness. And she was always coming up with something new, some wild and original thought which generated a long and sometimes heated discussion. She had a mind which, if he had been in the least insecure, would have caused some feeling of inadequacy, for not only was she the best in her specialty fields, she was the all-round woman, informed in fields where he had merely been briefed at some time or other during his continuing education.

Once, when he was younger, Don Duckworth had tried the traditional idea of marriage, and, although it worked for years, he was past the age to think in such terms. The fruit of his marriage, male and female, were, in his estimation, worthwhile people. His daughter was almost fifty now, and had, just before the *Maria* left Earth, received a government grant to do further research on the aging process. His son, just two years younger than his daughter, was engineer on board the *Nina*. He was quite proud of them, both of them, but he was seventy years old and they were so far away and, except for the rare meetings, no longer a part of his life.

Zees, he knew from past conversations, had chosen not to bear her allowed children. She had never consummated a contract of marriage. She had spent her young life in learning, had been a part of the survey teams on Venus and Mars. She had applied for and received sterilization at the age of eighteen years. He had taken his treatment after the birth of his son. With Ellen and Breed, it was the opposite. Ellen had produced her allowed two. Breed had not been married.

On the surface of it, the combination of their personalities seemed to indicate some problems, but the computers had been right. The half Indian and the tall redheaded woman, the seventy-year-old spaceman and the lady scientist, all worked, played, drank together.

The years aboard the *Maria*, where danger was not unknown, had made them a finely honed team, a unit, a sort of family unlike anything which had gone before. Early on it had become apparent that Ellen's nature included a liberal spicing of passion for that age-old man-woman game. Ellen liked variety and still teased Don into providing it now and then, but mostly it was Zees and Don, Ellen and Breed. It was a part of the human condition. In training no one talked of it much, but there were certainly no rules against it, either. Aboard the *Maria* sex was as much apart of life as the work and the eating and endless jumps.

And aboard the boat, in the dense and dark atmosphere of Worthless, Zees came to him and was woman and lay in his arms and talked the old, old dream of the wonderful lifezone planet and a release of the pressures of population on old Earth, and then they ate and speculated on the landmass below where fertile vegetation grew on the western and eastern coasts with the huge desert in the middle stretching southward to the mountains.

Computer pictures showed fernlike vegetation like something out of an imaginative illustration of a young Earth; and spot checks, from low altitude, gave them the feeling of steamy jungle.

When the biological monitors gave life readings in those woodlands they were tempted to search out that life, but both were disciplined people. There would be a time to chase after life—perhaps more of the type of animal he and Breed had seen dancing to an earthquake—after the survey was complete.

The mountains were truly awesome. Snow covered towering peaks. And to the south the treeline was often blasted by fire from the dozens of active volcanoes. There was, below the equator, an area of steamy hell where rank vegetation grew amid ravished burns and fields of hot lava. There the life signals did not appear. Giant fissures which would have made the Grand Canyon look shallow rent the tortured earth. The earth heaved and groaned with quakes and eruptions.

In the watery wastes of the southern ocean there were only the smoking and belching volcanoes, islands that formed and sank or blew apart in cataclysmic blasts.

The boat moved at speed, the small blink generator deinertializing the obstructing, dusty air, moving through the abrasive mixture without damage, as if in a vacuum.

They did not try to count the times they went around the planet, their path controlled by the computer so that instruments built a total picture of the surface.

The biological monitors showed, now and again, the signature of life below the warm waters of the southern ocean. On a spot check, lowering through cloud until, a hundred feet from the surface, they had eye contact with the water, they saw one form of life, an armored fishlike monster which showed clearly on the viewers as it surfaced, rolled sluggishly, and disappeared.

The ice at the south pole was lifeless. Zees sighed, the job almost complete. Breed's repair work was almost finished. "I see no reason to stick around," she said. "We couldn't ask anyone to live here. If the earthquakes didn't get them the volcanoes would. And sooner or later she's going to put herself in balance. She'll probably shift poles about ninety degrees, putting the poles where the equator is now."

"That," Don said, "would be one helluva ride."

"One I think I don't care to take," Zees said.

They slept. Sleep came slowly to Don. He was wondering if the *Nina* and the *Pinta* were having better luck, praying that they were.

Aboard ship, Ellen had been working with the biomonitors, tuning them to the signals which came mainly from the woodland areas of the northern landmass. It was time to take a look. The boat flashed back upward from the south and hovered over the eastern woodlands.

6

IN two years of exploration the crew of the *Maria* had found life. It was mostly vegetation and some low forms of bacteria. It existed on arid worlds, mainly. The vegetation on Worthless was more lush, more varied, and this, itself, was of interest. However, the burning desire of all, now that the survey was complete in regulation fashion, was to get another look at the little frog-kangaroo animal which had danced in an earthquake

As the boat lowered toward the steamy, fernlike forest, monitors and cameras worked, and the lack of variety in the vegetation disappointed Zees. On Earth, there were so many varieties of cacti alone that a catalog of types filled a six-volume set of books. The total number of life varieties discovered on all of the planets explored in over two years could be counted on the fingers of one hand. Worthless would swell the list, of course.

The biodetector aboard the boat was a delicate instrument which picked up electrical activity, lifestyle electrical activity. The signals given off by the frogroos, as Zees christened the little jumping animals, was a healthy bleep on the instrument as the boat hovered and the viewers occasionally caught sight of a frogroo through the obscuring vegetation.

Don put the boat down in a clearing where a frogroo was grazing on grasslike plants. The little beast was about as large as a cat, but in no way resembled a cat. Its skin was furred and tough-looking. It had long ears and a long snout and huge rear legs which were amazingly powerful. The animal in the clearing ignored the boat and continued to eat as it settled quietly. While eating, the frogroo went on all fours, hopping, using the shorter forelimbs as a fulcrum. When at last the frogroo noticed the boat, it stood tall on its rear legs for a moment, twitched its nose, then bounded away, seemingly not at all concerned.

Lesser life signals showed them a harelike creature of smaller size. From the boat, Ellen put them onto a stronger signal and Don lifted the boat and moved a few miles and came down near a bipedal, kangaroo type of animal browsing in a small glade near a stream. In many ways the larger animal resembled the frogroo. However, there seemed to be more refinement of form. The rear legs, for example, were straighter. Although still apparently capable of strong leaps, the rear legs were used to stand erect.

"An adult form?" Duckworth asked.

"I would be reluctant to say," Zees said. "There are similarities."

The animal stood quite near the boat, his forelimbs hanging, his long ears perked up. His eyes were double lidded, possibly, Zees pointed out, as a protection against the ever-present dust.

"He sees us," Duckworth said, as the boat's instruments recorded and measured.

"He's certainly not afraid," Zees said, as the animal began to walk toward the boat. He did not halt, but balanced himself by spreading his feet, when the earth shook.

The quake subsided. Don had kept his fingers on the controls, ready to lift if the quake became more severe.

"Look at old Longlegs," Zee said, thus giving the new animal a name.

Longlegs was making a slow and cautious approach. His alert eyes darted, his nostrils quivered, his ears twitched, moving as if to try to catch sounds from the boat. He stopped a few feet away. The ports seemed to interest him.

"Curious beggar," Don said.

"He's not afraid," Zee said. "That would seem to make him the dominant species on the planet. He's never seen anything to be afraid of before."

"The teeth of an omnivore," Don said.

Indeed, Longlegs was equipped with a fine set of teeth,

somewhat like a dog's teeth, with long fangs designed for holding and puncturing.

A stronger quake rumbled, the thunder of it heard even through the hull of the boat. Don lifted and hovered over the treetops.

"They seem to be coming closer together, the quakes," Zees said.

"Think we can risk going down again?" Don asked.

"I'd like to see more of Longlegs," she said.

Longlegs was waiting for them in the same clearing. Zees liked the looks of the animal. The round, double-lidded eyes were bright and intelligent-looking. The fur looked soft and warm. The little hands on the forelimbs were agile-looking. She would have liked to have a closer look, but the boat was not equipped for animal capture. She suggested that they step outside to see the animal's reaction.

Don went out first, a stun gun in his hand. The Longlegs had backed off when the port opened, but he did not flee when Don stepped out, heavy in his suit.

"All right, fellow," Zees said, although the sound of her voice did not go outside her helmet. "We're friendly."

Don had the stun gun ready. Zees moved a step forward. She put out her hands, and the Longlegs took a step backward.

"He seems gentle," Zees said.

"Maybe he thinks we're his breakfast," Don said, not liking the look of those teeth.

A strong tremor caused Zees to stumble. Longlegs balanced and seemed undisturbed by the earth movement. When the quake passed Zees took another step forward.

"What now?" Don asked.

Longlegs answered the question. He dropped to rest his weight on his short forearms, threw his head back, exposed his teeth and his soft, furry throat.

"That could be a challenge," Zees said.

"I have no idea," Don said, but he held the gun ready.

"Watch him," Zees said, leaning to put her gloved hands on the earth, throwing her head back. Longlegs repeated the movement.

"It's almost as if he is bowing to us," Zees said, standing.

"He doesn't seem to be agitated. Could exposing the vulnerable throat be a gesture of goodwill?"

"You do it," Zees said.

Don went through the hand-touching, bowing movement. Longlegs bowed back and then plucked a tuft of grasslike vegetation, moved slowly toward Zees. She took the grass from his hand.

"Fantastic," she said. "Don, pluck some for him."

Don selected the same sort of grass. Longlegs first bowed, then took the grass. He sat back on his haunches, gazing at them from his large eyes, and munched the grass contentedly. Finished, he bowed, then put both hands on Zees' shoulders. She did the same, standing there facing the slightly shorter animal, her gloved hands on the furred shoulders of Longlegs.

"If he's just proposed mating, you might be in trouble," Don said, with a chuckle.

There came the sound of distant thunder, a booming, eerie, low-pitched sound of violence. It came toward them with the speed of a rocket, and even then Don was moving, seizing Zees' arm, dragging her toward the boat.

The earth leaped under their feet as they started to run toward safety and they staggered as if drunk and they could see the force of the quake moving toward them in the form of a distinct wave in the trees and trees were falling, their crashing adding to the roar of approaching thunder.

Longlegs cavorted around them making sounds. His long ears twitched and pointed toward the approaching sound. Then it was upon them and they could not stand, fell heavily. The jungle floor heaved and trees crashed. Then there was a deadly silence.

The Longlegs was still dancing around them making sounds. He was also making frantic motions with his hands, and the long ears twitched, pointed toward the south. He would retreat toward the forest, come back, make waving motions with his hands, utter sounds from his mouth.

"It's as if he were trying to tell us something," Zees said.

"I think that quake was trying to tell us something," Don said. "It's saying let's get the hell out of here."

"Are you saying come with me?" Zees asked, her voice on the outside speaker of her suit.

Longlegs bowed, made frantic motions, moved toward the forest, looking back at them.

"Come on, Zees," Don said.

"Wait. Look." The animal was bowing, pointing toward the south, waving, one after the other. "He wants us to come. He's obviously agitated."

"The boat," Don said, pulling her along. Then he saw it. Two huge ferntrees had fallen, one from each side. Heavy branches lay across the boat. He ran ahead. The hull looked to be intact, but he could not get to the hatch, which he'd closed behind him. He tried to move a branch.

"It'll take an ax or something," he said, as Zees came to stand beside him. He activated his suit radio on the ship's frequency, knowing in advance that it was useless. He called and there was no answer. The units in the suits were designed for close work and did not have the power to reach up through the atmosphere to the *Maria*. However, when he missed his check-in, which would be due—checking his watch—in less than twenty minutes, then Breed would be down within an hour in the lifeboat.

Meanwhile, Worthless was going crazy. The thunderous rumble of quake came from the south again and he could see it coming and it was as bad as the first and Longlegs was going through his act, even more agitated than before.

"This fellow is intelligent," Zees said. "I get the distinct idea that he's trying to lead us to safety."

"I think we'd best stay with the boat," Don said. "The quakes are bigger and they're coming with more frequency, but this continent is relatively stable."

"He wants us to follow him," Zee said.

"It's probably only instinct. He's probably only trying to run away from the point of the quake's strength. And I'm still not sure he doesn't consider us edible."

"I'm going to follow, just a little way, to see if that's what he wants," Zees said, setting off.

Longlegs made a grimace which showed his teeth. Don, curious, followed Zees. When Breed came down in about an hour and a half they'd need to be near the boat, but there was some time to satisfy Zees' curiosity about the animal.

Longlegs seemed pleased. He cavorted ahead of them,

turning to wave them on. The ground began a rise, and the jungle changed character. Because the animal seemed so interested in their following him, Don went on, climbing. Rocks replaced the soft mulch underfoot, and still they climbed. They were a mile or so from the boat, but that didn't matter. When Breed landed he'd be in range of the suit radios.

The ferntrees thinned, gave way to a low brush, and then they were climbing rock, higher and higher. At the highest point they could see the desert ahead, stretching inland. Behind them they could see the top of the coastal jungle. A rare moment of clearing skies gave them the view and, to Zees, the planet took on a startling beauty. Sun glistened from the thick green of the jungle, and there, far away, she could see the jungle end and the ocean, also touched by the rare sun, glistened. She noticed a drop in temperature immediately as the suit compensated.

Longlegs had squatted on his haunches. His nose and ears pointed south.

"Is this it?" Zees asked him. He looked at her and there was something in his eyes. He was trembling. She put her gloved hand on his furred shoulder and he did not flinch. She rubbed and he glanced at her, showing teeth.

"He's trembling," she said to Duckworth. "I think he's afraid of something. Not us."

Longlegs turned toward her, pressed his soft muzzle against her suit, made a sound of unmistakable terror. It made shivers go up and down Zees' spine. She looked up, hoping to see the lifeboat lowering. Something was very, very wrong.

When the earth thunder began again it was the most terrible sound Zees had ever heard. Longlegs made that terrible sound of fright and sprawled to the ground, his fingers digging at the rock.

"Down," Zees said, flinging herself flat. Don was not fast enough and the earth did it for him, tossing his feet out from under him so that he landed heavily.

With the sound of thunder a world was in pain. The shifting of vast areas of the planet's crust shook the high mountains on their foundations.

From the *Maria,* Ellen and Breed had an overall view. They saw, via their instruments, the mountains heave and lose

their peaks as angular motion snapped loose millions of tons
of rock.

On the rise above the coastal jungle it was like riding a
roller coaster gone mad. The violent ups and downs were
unbelievable. And the entire planet seemed to groan in thunderous complaint. Below the rocky flatness on which the
three beings lay, clinging to bare rock, the jungle heaved and
rolled and the very earth was ruptured, letting the basin of the
jungle drop to send new clouds of dust into the air and
obscure the destruction of the boat.

The situation was too serious for Don to be terrified. He
was beyond terror. He was watching a cataclysm which no
man had ever seen, he was riding the crust of a world which
was trying to flip off its axis. He thought, for a while, as the
very rock leaped and dropped under him, that it was happening, and braced himself for an onrush of violent wind as the
world tipped and slipped inside her envelope of air to cause
vast airmass displacement.

And then the dust seemed to clear and there above them
was the sun and they could look out over the matted, destroyed jungle to see the ocean coming toward them.

The water seemed to come in slow motion, but the leading
edge of the high wall of water was racing, devastating what
remained of the fallen forest.

Longlegs bleated in fear. Don watched in awe as the wall
of water seemed to tower to the very heavens, and he reached
out, squeezed Zees' gloved hand, knowing that she, too, was
thinking that the water would overwhelm them, toss them,
crush them among the jagged and broken remnants of trees
and debris. Longlegs tried to run, but the dancing earth was
too much, even for him. He fell, tried to dig with his fingers.
And then the wall of water was near and not so tall and it
broke against the newly formed cliff and showered them but
left them alive.

Ellen was watching as the oceans moved over the northern
landmass. The pole had sunk, water swirled over ice and
covered it and rushed on to take the tundra. The shape of the
planet was changing before her eyes—or, to be more exact,
before the eyes of the ship's instruments. The series of huge
quakes, caused by massive movement of the crust, put the

weight of an ocean atop the topheavy northern hemisphere and the force transferred itself through the molten core to find release in the thin crust of the southern areas. Molten rock steamed tons of water, and the steam rose and filled the air and made the clouds more dense. New mountains grew within hours in the south, and the planet began to stabilize. The danger of her tipping on her axis seemed to be past.

Breed was with her, frantically trying to contact the boat by radio. Neither of them would speak of his fear. If the boat had been caught on the ground . . .

Zees and Don spent a lifetime on the high rise, and still it did not end. The ocean, tossed by the heaving crust, crashed again and again, and winds came to threaten them. They had moved slightly farther inland, crawling, grasping protruding rocks, and were sheltered in a shallow depression when the hurricane blew in from the sea carrying with it the debris which floated on the wild waters.

The air seemed to be more water vapor than air, and Longlegs, unprotected, was having difficulty. He sneezed repeatedly to clear his nares of the moisture. And then he screamed and Zees looked up to see a windblown branch piercing his body. The earth heaved and she could not reach him and his eyes were on hers, one set of lids closed making them look dim and dead.

It ended. Don breathed deeply inside his suit. He could hear Zees weeping quietly and looked—he'd been fascinated by the violence seen so dimly through the hurricane of wind—to see her kneeling beside Longlegs. The limb had been driven through the animal's chest. It was, unless the animal was capable of regeneration, a fatal wound. He could see that Longlegs was having trouble breathing, so he put a filtercloth over the snout. It didn't seem to help.

"Poor fellow," Zees said.

The eyes unlidded themselves, were, for a moment, bright and intelligent, and then it seemed as if the light had been switched off and Longlegs twitched, the eyes lidded, and he was dead.

They stayed on the high cliff beside the new sea. Aftershocks came, but they tapered off gradually. They were warmed by the suit heaters throughout a long, dark night. A new tidal wave came with morning, but did not reach them. Dust and smoke and steam had increased the denseness of the atmosphere so that they had visibility of only a few feet.

"Breed should be coming soon," Don said.

But the lifeboat would have to fly low over them to be within range of the suit radios.

Zees was moody. She nibbled space rations and drank water. She could not forget the look in the dying animal's eyes, a look of pure terror. He was dead. His body had stiffened overnight. She was a scientist. She used the suit's equipment to open him up. He was carbon-based life. His internal organs were surprisingly similar to those of a man, although he had double stomachs, one capable of long storage of food and water. When she was finished she knew a great deal about the Longlegs. She recorded her observations on the suit's small computer. Then she spoke to Don.

"He had one helluva brain," she said.

"Love those scientific terms," Don said, but he was looking up into the low clouds, hoping for a glimpse of metal. Now and then he'd open his radio to the ship's channel and send.

"It's a very well-developed brain," Zees said. "Longlegs has the potential to be anything we can be, if configuration of the brain has anything to do with it, if capacity has anything to do with it. And he knew what was happening. He was concerned for us. He saved our lives."

"Maybe the quakes didn't kill all of them," Don said. "If you're so impressed, maybe we'd better make contact with other Longlegs before we move on."

"All right," she said. "Now where the hell is Breed?"

She had a burning curiosity. She had experienced a moment or two, with Longlegs, when she felt as if the animal understood what she was saying. And the thought of encountering an intelligent being made her forget, for a moment, the reason for the Maria's long journey.

7

To Goroin Melt of Roag the warning tremors were nuisance,
nothing more. His body was dying under the combined onslaught of heart disease, age, dehydration, hunger. His vivid
rememberings had produced in his mind a state of near
nirvana which made the aches and pains of his body dimin-
ish. The central focus of his life force was the Great One. A
few earthpains could not divert his attention as he observed
the beast's increasingly frantic activity. The great eyes were
changing. Their fierce glow was being replaced by a kind of
dulled panic. In the natural order of his life the Great One
spent most of his waking hours browsing the desert.

Now Goroin could feel his moment approaching. It was
almost time. He would make his move in near darkness,
when poor visibility would aid the Great One's appetite in
overcoming natural caution. With the change so near, Goroin
gained renewed strength. He would make the final encounter
near the waterhole.

He rode out a heaving earthpain and then crawled over the
barrier. He moved slowly, using the boulders as cover. The
trip was a slow and torturous one. More than once he feared
that his overburdened heart would rupture, but he did not
abandon his care. To be seen by the Great One now, in full
light, could prove to be disaster.

He could feel the heat of the rocks on his hide. Rough
stones abraded him. He dragged protesting legs, and twice he
had to lie low as the Great One made futile exploration
around the canyon. Each time he saw the Great One his
admiration increased.

45

When at last he reached the cover of a pile of fallen boulders beside the pool of water, he lost consciousness for a time, and awoke to panic. When the Great One journeyed to the barrier he dragged himself to the water, rolled in it, drank deeply and, slightly revived, settled in to await the coming of twilight. The Great One prowled, roared, thrust his head into the water and blew cascades of spray, bellowed in hunger.

The final encounter would give new strength to the body of the Great One. And then Goroin the Great would push aside the puny barrier and trek to the western forests where there was food and forage in plenty, where he would wait and bide his time until the revenge of Roag the Rememberer was complete. Goroin Melt of Roag, Goroin the Great, would trumpet out the news.

When the Great One, near madness from hunger, tried to eat sterile stone he knew it was time. The beast, feeling the demands of his body, lifted the stones in his toothed mouth and the teeth made grinding, clicking sounds until, with a bellow of rage, the stone was ejected.

"Oh, World, be with me," Goroin prayed.

He showed himself. He crawled toward the waterhole. He allowed his failing body the last luxury of a drink, his eyes single-lidded, almost closed to hide the light of life.

Directly across from him the Great One crouched, his huge neck lowering. Huge and powerful legs, driven by days of fasting, bunched for the rush of capture. Goroin pretended to see the Great One for the first time, gave an animalistic squeal of terror and started a frantic, scrambling crawl, as if wounded. The Great One was still cautious, but through slitted eyes Goroin could see the gleam of hunger. With a bellow, the Great One launched his bulk into the water, sending up a mighty splash. He crossed the water with a speed which made Goroin want to yell in admiration.

Goroin, still pretending terror, crawled to the wall of the canyon and turned, at bay, helpless. The Great One's eyes were on him as the beast halted his rush only a short distance away. Caution made him undertake one last examination. Goroin closed his eyes quickly.

The moment was near. Goroin scuttled on all fours, back and forth, looking for escape, and the terrible teeth, the knowledge of the pain to come, gave a certain realism to his act, for he did know fear. He screamed with it, with the sure anticipation of the shock and the pain of those crushing jaws. He was not acting as he tried to dodge a thrust of the Great One's forepaw. He was sent rolling, and the power of the blow knocked the breath from him. He felt something break inside his chest and knew the stab of pain from broken ribs. He tried to crawl, screaming, saw the long, great, awesome neck pull back for the final strike. The breath of the Great One was hot on his face. The great mouth was open and the teeth were huge and sharp and deadly.

In his pain, Goroin had one coherent thought, over and above the knowledge that now it was time. He thought that had Roag ever faced such an eater there would have been no question of love. Only fear, awe, a huge pain in his chest.

The Great One would eat. Goroin's own Great One, perhaps the very last of the free-roaming Great Ones, would eat. The master of all Great Ones, so powerful, so invincible, so fearful, would now eat.

"Quickly, quickly," Goroin was praying as the earth heaved and groaned and dawn-age mountains fell and were lifted and the breakup of the high scarp ended Goroin's dreams of glory with a roar of falling stone which cascaded down from the wall of the canyon to smash the body of the Great One. The beast went down. His back was broken. He gave a final bellow of pain before another onslaught of falling stones quieted him forever.

Goroin, crouched against the wall of the canyon, was spared. The rock fall came within feet of him, and small debris peppered his startled, upturned face. And before his eyes the exposed head of the Great One moved feebly. The great eyes opened, stared, and then took on the dullness of death.

Goroin's wail of pure anguish was lost in the continued roar of earth thunder, and then he fell, lying as dead himself, the pain of broken ribs adding to the protest of his hurt heart. And still the earth pained and rocked and fell and jerked and Goroin was only half aware of the greatest earthpains of his experience.

In a silence he opened his eyes. There was a sadness in

him. Now he would know Roag's despair, the waste of melting, for he was wounded, near death in body, and the earth had changed. Around him there was only the wilderness of the desert, and, even if he had possessed the strength of body to conduct another long search, the chances of finding another Great One were nonexistent. The last of the free Great Ones was dead.

He did not have the strength to fight the inevitable. He could feel bone grating in his chest when he breathed. He clung to the dying body through dint of will.

He slept.

He awoke to the memories of Roag, the sure knowledge that he, Goroin, now faced Roag's fate, an eternity of not being. And the fear of it gave him the strength to crawl. The Great One's tongue had been forced from his mouth. It was still hot. He ripped it away and chewed. Hot blood gave him strength. He ate more as he crawled, and climbed, and hurt, and prayed. There was one feeble hope. There was animation in the desert, mostly insignificant creatures. He could even hope that the severe earthpains had so disoriented a springer that it had wandered into the desert.

He had eaten half of the hot, nourishing tongue. He saved the rest. He would not give up as long as his body could move. He reached the barrier, what was left of it, crawled painfully over it, gained his two feet and staggered away from the much-altered scarp, having to detour around a new chasm opened by the vast earthpains.

When the final paroxysm of the planet came he was at a distance from the scarp, but was almost overwhelmed by the massive fall of stones which made the once-impressive cliffs sloping piles of rubble. The uplands of the desert rode the waves of force, tossing him as he lay full length and tried to cling with feet and hands to the world gone mad. He survived. He survived, it seemed, only to suffer. His body was going stiff. It was as if parts of it were already dead. He could move only by using his forelimbs for balance, like the newest-born springer. Each movement cost him a price in pain. He saved the remaining tongue, stored it in his upper stomach, drew on it now and again for moisture and nourishment.

Around him the desert seemed to be lifeless. He knew that the eastern woodlands were much too far away to be reached in his condition. He did not rest. He knew that if he halted he would never rise again. When he fell heavily he crawled. He crawled in darkness of night, and the dawn overtook him at the edge of a giant new fissure. The detour around that fissure took the last of his hope. He had no further reserves of strength.

At midday he fell and could not rise. He lay on his stomach, his forelegs moving feebly, trying to draw his leaden body forward. He lost all hope then, let his heavy eyes close, bade farewell to life, to Melin of Grace, to all of his dreams. He did not, at first, hear the approach of the small eater. When he did hear the movement he forced one eye open and saw a food creature, small, insignificant.

The World was kind. That small food creature, good only for a rather unsatisfying meal, was knowing hunger. Goroin did not move. He lay as if dead, knowing that the creature was a scavenger, a cowardly animal by nature, living mainly on vegetation and not often having a meal of flesh. He was, after all, not in a position to choose. The eastern woodlands were still far away and he was unable to move. He was dying and the food creature was his chance.

Love the eater? He knew an unholy hate as the cowardly little beast sniffed and started, almost ran, came sneaking back, sniffed again. For a long time he thought the beast was too frightened to eat, and then he felt the nibble of sharp little teeth at the point of thin fur surrounding that with which he had so joyfully blended with Melin of Grace. His first urge was to strike out and kill the cowardly animal, but he felt his heart give a huge beat and felt it tearing and he quickly flowed to the point where the creature was now ripping and tearing, having tasted blood. He awaited the moment, concentrated his force, felt the tearing teeth and flowed with a swoop.

Goroin Melt of Roag looked for a sad moment at the dead flesh before his small eyes. Then he continued to eat. He was hungry. He tore into the soft insides of flesh and glutted himself, until his low-slung belly protruded. Then he drank of the still-warm blood.

There was a lithe and wiry strength in the new body. He knew shame, but at least he was alive and unmelted. At least he had been given a new opportunity to seek. There would be springers in the woodlands. And if he should encounter any of the free people en route he would avoid them. The mere thought of encountering Melin of Grace while in the form of a food creature was a pain which made him weep.

Goroin Melt of Roag, so nearly Master of the Great Ones, trotted in a small, carrion-eating body, the accumulated knowledge of the people in the form of a food creature. A wave of pure hate savaged him. Moulan the Strong still ruled, and would rule forever. He hated himself. He hated the shades of Roag. He hated the last of the free-roaming Great Ones for dying in the very moment of Goroin's glory. He hated his people, those who served the tyrant, Moulan. He hated the free people for not opposing Moulan.

He trotted toward the eastern woodlands. And into his deeply emotional state came awareness of a difference in the world. There was moisture in the air, and more dust. He coped with it by using hair filters in his nares. He knew that severe earthpains had occurred, but he had no conception of the seriousness of what had happened. He had no knowledge of anything beyond his own experience, and the shades of experience left by Roag.

At least he had not melted. There was a youthful energy in him. He found himself enjoying the feeling of floating when he leaped. He decided that any life, however insignificant, was preferable to nonlife, to melting. He wasted a couple of days getting to know his body, although he had no intention of remaining with it for long. He ate of the sparse vegetation, chased and devoured a tiny animal which he would once have scorned as not even a mouthful.

After all, there was now no pressing hurry. His choice was clear. He would seek a springer, be eaten. Then would come the long period of self-training, of growth.

He could even find some good in it. Melin of Grace was younger. Before she aged and had to seek a new beginning he would be able to grow the new springer body into adulthood and find her. Then, together, they could seek. Perhaps this time he could persuade her to go with him. Perhaps, beyond the devastated scarp, on the rising slopes of the mountains, there were other Great Ones.

He stored new knowledge seen from the level of the desert ground and moved in the general direction of the eastern woodlands.

8

ELLEN Partance was on watch when the first of the mountain-building convulsions hit Worthless. She knew something big was happening when instruments began to go wild. She called down to Breed, who was about neck deep in a blink converter. Breed was on the bridge within a couple of minutes, and his first action, when he realized what was happening, was to leap to the radio. There was no need for rules of radio communication. In some four or five hundred years the weak signals from the *Santa Maria*'s radio would reach the vicinity of Earth, and by that time Breed would be in no position to care if his words were monitored and a reprimand issued.

"What the hell's going on down there, Don?" Breed yelled. "Don, do you hear me?"

"They had landed," Ellen said. She was trying not to look worried. But through her instruments which sent various waves to penetrate the muck that was the planet's atmosphere she'd seen mountains being demolished, others being raised in a long and jagged rent in the planet's crust.

"The damned thing didn't tip, did it?" Breed asked.

"No," she said. "But the eastern forest area sank, and the ocean rushed in."

"They got away," Breed said. "They had to get away. Maybe the new stuff in the atmosphere is blocking radio signals."

"Maybe they're down low, getting a good look at it all," Ellen said. "They were here, Breed." She pointed to the exact spot on the computer-built map.

52

Breed tried the radio again, left the channel open. "Have you tried the biomonitor?" One thing about a man, using the term generically—he put out a helluva signal. The ship's biomonitor should be able to spot two human systems easily.

"Sorry, I didn't think," Ellen said, leaping toward the control console. She pushed buttons. Breed came to stand beside her. He frowned as she shook her head in puzzlement.

"I'll check the breakers," he said, and dived behind the console, came up. "They're all OK."

"Breed, all that volcanic and earthquake activity has played havoc with the planet's magnetosphere," Ellen said.

Breed hummed a little as he checked instruments. The biomonitor and other monitors continued to give erratic and meaningless readings. As he worked the chaos continued on the planet below.

"They were self-tuned," he said, "in relationship with the electromagnetic field on the planet. A few segments of the computer blew when they tried to keep up with the rapid changes."

"Can you fix it?" Ellen asked.

"Sure," he said. "The question is, how long will it take?"

"Come on, Breed," she said. "You're scaring me."

"Well, honey, I'm a little scared myself. Take a look." He switched up a test panel. There were almost a hundred trouble lights showing in the diagram of the computer's monitoring system.

He began his work. Down below the planet gradually settled down. There were mountains where there had been oceans. There were oceans where there had been land. A new covering of ash was sifting down on the southern hemisphere, although volcanic activity, after the big blowup, had lessened greatly. The instruments which penetrated to the surface and drew maps were busy, and early tracings showed titanic changes. Perhaps the most serious change of all, from the point of view of people who wanted to make Worthless a home for people, was the additional burden of ash, dust, water vapor, and other volcanic debris in the already dense air. In spite of their worry about Don and Zees, Breed and Ellen were somewhat awed, for they had just seen, they realized, the first moment of an ice age. The planet would not freeze over in a matter of days. It would be a long and gradual icing. She still had her internal heat, but the weak sun, not far enough along in its evolutionary cycle to give sufficient warmth, would be blocked completely from the surface. The greenhouse effect, created when the atmosphere allowed penetration of the sun's energy and trapped it there under the cloud layers, would no longer function, for now the energy of the star would not penetrate.

It had all been for nothing. They'd spent time investigating and hoping for worth in a planet which had been next to Worthless and now was absolutely Worthless. And unless they heard from Don and Zees soon, each of them felt, without vocalizing it, that it would have all been for less than nothing, for a net loss, for a soul-shattering personal loss of two people who had been a part of their unique little "family."

"Don, do you hear? Zees, speak to me." Ellen was on the radio. In return she got nothing, just the slight hiss of nothingness, the lonely, eternal sound of deep and empty space.

"I'm going down," Breed said, halting his testings of tiny things inside the computer. He had seen quickly that repairing the monitor circuits would be the work of days, perhaps even weeks.

"Not without me," Ellen said, and there was something in her voice which caused him to abort his half-formed reply that she should stay on the ship. He knew how she felt. With Don and Zees missing she did not want to be alone.

"If something should happen, I'd want to be with you," she said.

And again he read her thoughts behind the statement. Meaning, he thought, that you would not want to be alone out here.

"Right," he said. "Get suited up."

The second and last small vehicle stored neatly into the *Maria*'s cargo and engine areas was designed for emergencies. It was equipped with a small blink generator and navigation equipment. It did not have the scientific instruments of the close-in exploration boat. It was a lifeboat, a way out, a way home. There were concentrated rations for four to last six months. Theoretically, any distance which had been lined by blink beacons could be covered in the lifeboat in much less time than that.

The *Maria*, clicking and humming to herself, her automatics having been given a last check by Breed, closed her hatch behind them upon an electronic order from the lifeboat. Ellen, looking back at her through a rear viewer as the lifeboat sank down toward the roiling atmosphere of the planet, thought she looked lonely.

9

SNUG in their suits, with air and food and water to last quite long enough for Breed to come pick them up, Zees and Don Duckworth spent the first day in the immediate area of the small depression in the rocky desert where their friend the Longlegs had died. During the day they saw several of the frogroos. The little animals seemed to be disoriented. However, they noted that there seemed to be a gradual movement of the small animals toward the south.

The day was not a total waste. Zees recorded observations, used the gear included in her suit to make some soil checks. However, the desert offered little variety. She moved toward the south, along the new coastline, keeping in touch with Don via the suit radios. There she discovered, not over a mile from their site, that a small portion of forest had survived on a slope leading down toward the sea.

The native life of the forest had suffered terribly. She found a mangled frogroo almost immediately. A quick study showed the animal to be, indeed, a juvenile form of Longlegs. She called Don to join her. There were several living frogroos moving about in the shattered forest, and she caught a quick glimpse of another type of animal which looked a lot like an Earthside rabbit.

Don joined her. He sadly dispatched an injured frogroo trapped by a fallen tree and too mangled to live.

Astoundingly, there was no insect life. And in a day of exploring the small tract of forest, moving through it laboriously over fallen trees and piled debris, only the two previously noted types were seen. They were both saddened to find a dead Longlegs. There were some minor differences in the two dead Longlegs. The second one, smashed severely in the fall of trees, had white hair around its long snout and slightly shorter ears, and the coloring was of a lighter hue than the fur of the first Longlegs.

It was puzzling to Zees to find only two basic sizes of the animals, the small frogroos and the much larger Longlegs, and yet, internally, there was no doubt that they were the same species.

Don speculated that when the frogroos matured past the size which was common, they migrated out of the forest areas.

All three life types had one thing in common, the teeth of the omnivore. The rabbitlike animal was seen eating carrion. The frogroos browsed upon vegetation.

In addition to the lack of insects there was one other form of life conspicuous by its absence. A total lack of reptile and bird life raised some interesting questions about evolution on Worthless. Without reptiles, the leap from one-celled life to the mammal stage would have been by a different route than that taken on Earth.

They passed time by discussing the possibilities. And after their third night on the planet it was time to discuss another subject. Where were Breed and Ellen?

Don could think of no reason why they had not been picked up immediately. If the lifeboat had not come within radio range, all the others had to do was check the biomonitor and sent the lifeboat directly to the unmistakable signal put out by the human body.

Zees did not allow herself to worry. The instruments on board the *Maria* were the finest. She knew that Breed and Ellen would risk all, if necessary, to find them.

The thought which kept coming back to Don was that somehow the titanic convulsions on Worthless had affected the *Maria* herself. She was orbiting not too far above the atmosphere.

At fifty-five, Zees was in the prime of her life. She was a very feminine woman, softly curved, but with hardened and conditioned muscles and reflexes. She had been through worse than spending a few days in a suit. Once she had fallen victim of the ancestor-tracing fad, and had been able to determine that she was a product of the western migration of the nineteenth century, going back to a participant in one of the Oklahoma land rushes. Her formative years had been spent in the relatively uncrowded hot deserts of the southwest. Her father had owned two of the few horses which were living outside zoos. She had become interested in animals early, and had added a degree in zoology to her half-dozen degrees in the field of geology and chemistry.

After she'd had enough of schools, she entered the Space Service and scored so high on all tests that she became a part of the early survey teams which found both Mars and Venus to be, like the planet upon which she now walked, worthless.

Among her minor interests was the ancient myth-science of astrology, and she liked to think of herself as a typical Gemini. On one plane, she was the seeker of knowledge, the archetype of the new scientist, with interests and knowledge in many fields. Had she chosen to apply her abilities to the private sector, she would, no doubt, have been quite wealthy. On another plane of the twin personality, she was, first and foremost, woman, and pleased to be. She liked the way she looked, although she knew her own faults. She honed her body into shape with a study of ballet and modern dance. She was not smug about herself, but she rather liked being Zees. She liked men for the way they were, and she in particular liked Don Duckworth. If she had to be marooned on a planet, she could think of no better fellow maroonee.

During the night following the third day it was necessary to discuss their situation. Like Zees, Don had been in tight places before. Once he had crash-landed on the moon in a test vehicle with a punctured hull and less than a day's supply of air in his suit. He was not a man to panic easily. He had faith in the hardware on the *Maria,* and most of all he had faith in his crew.

"I'll say only that there must be a very good reason why they haven't come," he said.

"I'm a bit disappointed," Zees said. She, too, had faith in Breed and Ellen. She would not admit her worst fear, that something final and quite deadly had happened on *Maria.* "I think it's time we started conserving rations."

"What rations?" Don asked. He'd been so sure that Breed would be along at any time that he'd made no effort to conserve the food inside his suit. He was, of course, not concerned about water. The suit's reclamation unit handled that without appreciable loss.

"So what now?" Zees asked.

"I can afford to lose a little weight," Don said. "A day or two without food won't hurt either of us."

"Don," she said.

"I know, I know," he said, still reluctant to even talk about it. "So I'll say it if you want. If worst comes to worst the air can be breathed. We can filter it. The flesh of those small animals—"

She knew more about that than he, having dissected one of the frogroos. "Yes," she said. "Unless there's some basic biological booby trap there which I can't see."

"We have a couple of days," Don said. "I can't imagine anything's going wrong with the ship or the instrumentation which Breed can't jury-rig to work in that length of time."

"I think I'd like to do some exploring," Zees said.

"Yeah, it'll give us something to occupy the time."

They walked.

"If we should have to try to live off the land we'd do better to stick to the forest," Zees said, after hours of walking across the desert.

"I have the urge to see what's beyond that next hill," Don said lightly. He wanted to put off opening the suits as long as possible.

They saw one or two of the rabbitlike creatures, and they seemed to be quite shy. On the other hand, the frogroos of the forest allowed close approach, close enough for the use of the suit's weapons.

They walked for one day into the desert, into an unchanging and dimly seen barrenness. Once Zees saw a richness of gold on the surface, a large, exposed vein of it. They spent the night in the desert, and with the dim light of the new day decided that it was time to return to the cliff overlooking the sea, the spot nearest to the last location known to Breed and Ellen.

The recycled air within the suits was growing stale. They

limited their activity. Another day passed, and another night. And when evening's darkness began to come Don decided that it was time. "Stand by," he said, "to restart the cycler if I black out or anything."

He closed off the cycler, opened his vent, adjusted the filters in his mask to sweep out the dust particles in the air. "Here goes," he said.

It was like breathing pure oxygen, after having lived with the stale air in the suit for so long. "My God," he said.

"What's wrong?" Zees asked, her hand flying to his cycler controls.

"It's so rich," he said. "It almost makes you drunk."

He lived on the air of Worthless through the night, and in the morning she joined him in breathing the oxygen-rich mixture. It made her feel heady, almost happy.

It would have been easy to lose track of time. The nights were black, but the days were only slightly less murky. And their enforced fast was having an effect. Zees was feeling light-headed. The fierce hunger of the first three days without food was gone, and in its place was a feeling of detachment. She merely nodded when Don said that it was time to make another decision.

Neither of them had the heart to kill one of the playful, happy frogroos. He chose one of the rabbit things, setting his weapon to merely stun. The charge was deadly to the small animal.

The exploration suits were packed with marvelous equipment. In Zees' suit were tools which made a small portable laboratory. Don's suit was equally amazing in its complexity, but neither came equipped with matches. There was no way to make a fire. Don tried striking sparks with a flintlike rock and failed miserably.

Zees had cleaned the small animal with her dissecting tools. The flesh looked clean and edible. She shrugged. Don watched, a look of distaste on his face, as she bared her white teeth and bit into a leg. It tasted like cold raw steak. She chewed. Don started to follow suit but she made him wait for four hours, made him watch her ingest a small portion of the meat and await any negative reaction. When she survived, and, indeed, hungered for more, they dined.

It was food. It was raw and it needed salt but it was food. They washed it down with reclaimed water. The small animals, although shy, were plentiful. They would not starve. They could use the suit's water system to filter water clean. The air was a joy, rich, heady. "Things are looking up," Zees said, as she settled back to sleep, out of the suit for the first time in days, using it for a pillow. She slept well and dreamed of a heavenly planet with clear skies and good water and fruit trees.

Another day. Don, the great white hunter, said that he'd go provide breakfast. As it turned out, he did not have to leave the spot where Zees lay, still drowsy. He saw one of the little rabbity things coming closer, as if it were curious.

"They're really cute little things," Zees said. "Shame to kill it."

"Yes," Don said, lifting his weapon. He'd lowered the charge still further, for there'd been a bit of overkill on the last one. He let the animal take a few more hops and then, just as it seemed that the animal saw them, he pressed the trigger. He felt a moment of curious regret. But a man had to eat.

10

GOROIN Melt of Roag was adjusting surprisingly well to being small. He no longer felt shame. He had a natural curiosity about his world, and seeing it from the eyes of a food creature was a new experience. He was in no hurry to reach the zone of woodlands. He drank the dew of the mornings and ate of the tough vegetation. He covered ground with an effortless ease which led to many side excursions of exploration. He was rewarded by finding a new spring of pure water which had been formed after the upheaval. He drank deeply and wallowed playfully.

There was, he noted, a difference in the earthpains. When they came their intensity was low. In all the days of travel he had not once been forced to halt and cling to the earth. He also noted that the nights seemed to be cooler. His world had changed. He did not have the knowledge to know the seriousness of that change. He ate well, drank at his newly discovered spring, and then set out, determined to make a day's march of the remaining distance to the woodlands. He moved with a steady, ground-eating pace, and to break the monotony he did mind exercises, reviewing all his lore. Thus occupied, he almost ran into two strange creatures.

The concept of alien beings was not in his frame of reference. Although he had never seen animals like the two tall, bipedal things, each of which had one huge, reflecting eye which extended almost all the way around its head, they were on his world and, therefore, of his world. On his world there were certain rules. Rule number one was that the people had long since exterminated the great carnivores, which had been their only competition.

Goroin did not feel fear at seeing the two strange creatures. He began immediately to dream dreams. He had lost the chance to be Goroin the Great, in the form of the most admirable Great One he'd ever seen, but there was new opportunity. Here was an animal a bit larger than the long-legged form of the people. Their movements seemed to be slightly awkward, but he noted with satisfaction that the thick, heavily skinned arms were instruments of a certain precision. The thickness of the animals' bodies indicated strength. And, most important, there was no glow of life in the huge single eye.

They had not yet seen him. He used natural ground cover to observe, and to sneak closer. Strange that he'd never seen such animals before. Perhaps they had, during the huge earthpains, migrated up from the zone of fires. It was a logical conclusion, since the skin of the animals seemed to be capable of resisting heat. It had a slick, hard look, and yet it was flexible and moved as they moved.

Still, he was small, and caution was required. He watched. He could feel no hunger coming from the two animals, and that concerned him. He decided to show himself. They moved too slowly to be able to catch him if he did not want to be caught. He widened his eyes to show his life glow, and there was no retreat on the part of the animals. Perhaps they had never encountered life. That was to the good. He capered closer, teasing them. There was some interest now, for they both turned their large eyes toward him.

Yes, he wanted one of those strange, strong-looking bodies. He made his decision. He pretended not to see the animals and casually approached them. He had a feeling of sheer joy. The World had not deserted Goroin Melt of Roag when it tossed some of its stones down atop his Great One. The World provided.

"Come," he was saying, "come, have a little feast, my friend." He favored the larger one. And, pleasingly, it was the larger one who had tensed and was watching him.

He got a faint hint of hunger. Ah, yes. "Come, come," he urged. And then he screamed as the large animal lifted a hand which held an object which was not familiar to him, for in that moment he had achieved the right angle to see without reflection and he saw two living eyes behind that outer shell of eye and even as he screamed and leaped he was hit by the World and he fell heavily, lay limply and helplessly, his eyes unmoving but still seeing as the animal with the living eyes came, bent, picked him up.

He was dead, but he lived. He was fully aware and he was incapable of movement. He saw the sharp claw extended from the end of the hand of one of the animals and felt the sharpness slice through his throat and his blood began to drain in a red rush of heat. And there was life in the eyes of the animals. Life.

He was faced with two terrible choices. He could flow out of the body of the food creature with the blood and float free to melt, to lose all, to drift until, after perhaps eons of times, he accidentally lodged within life. Then he would be only a shade; Goroin Melt of Roag would be melted and no more. In all of his knowledge he knew of no double melt. How far could life be extended? Did it have the power to survive two melts? It was a risk he dared not take.

On the other hand if he was eaten and flowed into the eater there he would face madness. There he would face the horror of two life units fighting for control. He knew of that through the memories of Roag, who had seen the starving carnivore, who had freed two life units by blinding the animal and killing it with a stone.

His decision had to be made quickly. It had happened so suddenly. He considered the sadness of not being, and his fighting spirit surged up. He would, since the eater was obviously unsuspecting, assault that life form with all his power. He would surge in and strike and, in surprise, perhaps dominate. Perhaps he could avoid madness. At least by fighting he had some hope. He could not bring himself to abandon all in a melt.

He, being an eater himself, knew that the haunch of the food creature was choice meat. Just before the rear legs were severed from the body he flowed and concentrated himself there. He lodged in fleshy softness and waited and drew his power into a tight little knot ready to unleash it. He transferred on the first bite into flesh. He flowed, felt the powerful, grinding teeth. He knew the mobile tongue and then he was seeking and finding and surging up the flow lines and assaulting a brain with all his force to be absorbed and blinded and encapsulated in nothingness.

He screamed as it hit him from all sides, vast balls of roaring fire in nothingness, a world spinning as if dizzy, things moving through nothingness and a sun which covered all the sky and the earth with light and clean, white clouds and tastes and smells and sounds and a knowledge of femaleness as the vast store of knowledge in the brain of Zees swept over him in a numbing wave.

Zees felt a sudden dizziness. She breathed deeply and lifted her faceplate to wipe her face. She sat down.

"Something wrong?" Don asked.

"No." Because she was fine now, just that one moment of dizziness.

Goroin had been overwhelmed. He whimpered as the madness continued to sweep over him. Smooth-skinned animals and exploding novas and a complicated language and lust and a vast universe made of tiny things, atoms, and the air consists of and the feel of the food in mouth and alcoholic drunkenness and all of the billions of impressions stored within a human brain and the world, his world, seen from a vast distance, all was dumped on him in one indigestible mass and he screamed and fought and was trapped, blocked.

"You look as if you're not feeling well," Don said.

"Just a headache," Zee said. She triggered the medical kit inside the suit, felt the slight sting of spray injection. "I guess everything is just catching up with me, Don."

"Better?" he asked, after a few moments.

The drug was taking effect.

Calmness began to soothe the maelstrom of madness, and he could see, could see his own world through a pair of very efficient eyes. He could hear. But he was blocked away. Was this madness? He rested. He closed himself away, shut out the confusion. He looked inside himself and he was there, and the shadow of Roag. And a terrible thought came to him. Had Roag been trapped inside him as he was now trapped, had he known and been unable to free himself for all this time?

He fought wildly. There was no way out.

There was something wrong. She felt weak, and the headache, in spite of medication, would not go away. "Don, I think I'm having a reaction to something," she said.

"Button up the suit and let the monitor have a look," Don said.

She closed off and breathed the stale air of the suit's system. She activated the medical monitor, and Don read. Her pulse was up just a bit, her heartbeat a bit fast. Her blood pressure was normal. A tiny needle took a blood sample, and the sample underwent basic analysis. Her blood sugar was down, as was to be expected after days of fasting and an all-protein diet. There were no infections.

"Tension?" Don asked.

"Perhaps," she admitted.

"I prescribe a rest," Don said.

She leaned against a rock, having once again opened the suit to breathe the filtered air. She had always been able to sleep when opportunity presented itself. It was a protective learned characteristic of all who worked in space. She closed her eyes and thought pleasant thoughts and felt sleep coming.

When outside stimuli ceased to be thrust upon Goroin along with the collected impressions of several decades, the burden on his sanity was eased. He began to recover. He collected himself. He was still Goroin Melt of Roag. He did not reach out in suddenness and panic, knowing the trauma of that. He extended himself slowly, studying and mapping. He explored a synapse at a time and accumulated knowledge.

It was a fantastic brain. It was beautifully complicated. And the knowledge it contained! Not madness. Order. The breathtaking concept of a limitless universe, the galaxy as seen from the great emptiness, spreading out in glory. He flowed faster and faster. He became a part of it. If he had encountered human culture in his own form he would have been a victim of cultural shock, but now he was human. He was much like a baby, learning, but learning at a pace never matched by a human infant. He was traveling all the intricate pathways of a human brain and had the ability to know things which Zees herself had forgotten. He reveled in it. He knew, within minutes, more than the accumulated stored knowledge of all his people. He had a concept of time and paused a moment to relate it to his own experience. By his best estimate he was thousands of years old. Then onward. Power. These creatures had the power to destroy a world. Incredible power, power to make Moulan the Strong a helpless thing. One blast from one of the weapons and Moulan would be carrion.

Before Zees awoke, Gorion Melt of Roag had shared everything which she was. And still he was a prisoner. He had not been able to penetrate that vital portion of her which, for example, controlled will, controlled the motor areas. There was a part of her which was inaccessible to him, but he was no longer in panic.

In that very brief time Goroin learned more about the human brain than was known by all of Earth's medical scientists, and while he admired the complexity of it he also recognized its main weakness.

Goroin had known three types of brains—the empty and malleable brain of a springer, waiting to be developed and formed by an infusion of life; the fully developed brain of the form called by the humans Longlegs; and the smaller but efficient brain of a food creature. Each of the brains he had inhabited was completely utilized. Each of them had the same basic components, and all components were used. This human brain seemed to have been formed in a wasteful manner, for large areas of it were not utilized to their potential.

The irony of it was that this species, these humans, while having made long strides in fields of knowledge, did not know itself. One of his people, using the entire facilities of a lesser brain, had superior assets in many ways. These humans, for example, relied on a spoken language, a concept which, before he, himself, became human, had not existed on the world which the humans called Worthless.

Goroin had free access to areas of minimal utilization. He was lodged primarily in one complex which, as far as he could determine, was inaccessible to his host's mind. He was no longer afraid. He was too interested. He shared the perceptions of his host without ability to influence mind or body, but there was hope. The life force of this human was there, somewhere, and still unsuspecting. He would find a way to reach it. And with the advantage of surprise, he would dislodge, control, push the human back into the areas where he was now trapped. Unless he read the life force wrong, it was relatively weak.

He experienced Zees' great joy when, suddenly, a voice came over the suit radios.

"Breed," Don Duckworth said calmly, "where the hell have you been?"

"I've probably flown directly over you a hundred times," Breed said.

"What's the problem?" Zees said.

"I just discovered that the altered magnetic field of the planet was messing up radio, too. I had to adjust frequencies on a random pattern to find the right one. It took time."

"Yeah, we know," Don said.

"Coming down," Breed said. 'See me yet?"

Visibility was less than two hundred feet. But then the lifeboat swam down into view, a huge, metallic glistening in the mottled dark clouds which looked, roiling, as if they were alive. "Got you," Don said. "Bring her on down. There's a nice level spot right under you."

During the excitement of getting aboard the lifeboat Goroin was able to send one tiny stimulation. He caused a set of nerves just over Zees' right eye to twitch once. He was encouraged. Then he was lost in wonder as he saw through Zees' eyes the cloud-shrouded ball which was the World. He felt the stimulation of alcohol, the kisses of greeting. He came to know the humans called Breed and Ellen. He ate the ship eagerly, questing with his mind to go over all Zees knew of its operation

The body of Zees-Goroin slept comfortably. A thorough medical check had shown no ill effects from the stay on the planet. Goroin did not sleep. He explored. He probed. He learned. All he had to do was find a way to break through and the ship would be his, the World would be his. The universe, ah, noble concept, would be his.

Having the family all together again called for a celebration. Breed took time off from repairing the computer. He had finished declouding the chamber of the generator. A unanimous vote put the last real, nonfabricated Earthside steak on the table along with a bottle of real wine. The steak and wine had been saved to be used in celebration of finding a real Earth-type planet, but having Don and Zees returned from the dead was reason for celebration, too.

After the meal they moved to the recreation room and sampled the ship-made booze liberally. Zees told the others about the interesting form of life on the planet, the Longlegs. Ellen pretended to be interested, but, the emotion of having found her friends alive having passed, she was on a downer. Half the provisions aboard *Maria* were gone. They'd have to start back toward Earth now, and she felt pessimistic about the chances of finding a lifezone planet.

It was agreed that a lifeboat trip should be made back to the planet, when Breed got the biomonitors working, to get a close look at Longlegs, to determine if he really was an intelligent species.

Zees was having odd little flashbacks. For no reason at all she'd be remembering some insignificant event far in the past. Once, while listening to Don talk about a possible route to be taken when the trip back toward Earth began, she was suddenly walking in open desert, five years old. She could smell the desert air, feel the heat, see the delicate bloom of a cactus. It was almost as if she were there to see a desert lizard scuttle away. Then she was reciting the periodic table and not missing a single division. She was familiar with the damned thing, but she'd never tried to memorize it. She could see it in her mind from top to bottom.

"I'd say a week or so should be enough time to study Longlegs," Don said. "Then we'll be off. "There's an interesting area of dense star formation around Delphinus."

"I'm sure that the Longlegs who led us to the safety of the rocks was communicating," Zees said. "It was primitive communication, of course, but more than animal behavior."

"If he's intelligent," Breed said, "he'll either start growing a thicker fur coat or find a way to get off Worthless."

"Why?" Zees asked.

"Because in a relatively short geological time that planet is going to be an ice ball," Breed said.

She hadn't thought of it. It was in her field and she hadn't thought of it. It was logical. The extra density of the atmosphere after the wild cataclysm. Sun heat blocked.

Goroin was shocked into stillness. His world frozen? A vast field of ice from pole to pole? Oh, World.

Zees thought about the happy frogroos, the Longlegs, and was sad.

Sad? Goroin was devastated. All animation would die. All life would melt, float free, and there would be no animate body, no hope, only eons of floating, and if animal life ever did develop again on Worthless there was no guarantee that the floating, melted life forces would have been able to exist through the endless centuries of frozen death. He dreamed wild dreams of taking the people away, but the *Santa Maria* was small, would hold no more than a few, and from his host's mind he knew the difficulty of finding other livable planets. To Earth? Humans crowded that planet with their teeming billions. The people would be overwhelmed. And it was so far, so far. Build other ships? No time. Not even with the abilities of all four humans could he expect to develop Worthless into an industrial planet before the glaciers began to push down and up from the poles.

After sleep Zees joined Breed in the repair of the computer. Her guest learned the principles of electronics, and the astoundingly simple physical laws which allowed the miracle of old Jonathan Blink to reduce limitless space to nothing.

Goroin could now cause several reactions in Zees' body. He could make her scratch a spot near her eye. He could surface hidden memories. He could, and this was a new achievement made possible, in part, by the natural thirst of a hangover, cause the body to thirst. After sending Zees to take water twice in a quarter hour he abandoned that practice as being counterproductive.

It took two days only to make the monitor system operational. Meanwhile, Worthless was showing signs of becoming more and more stable. Volcanic activity in the south was still interesting but not earthshattering. Zees did some calculations. The drift of the landmass would continue; an ice age was definitely in the offing. She could not make an accurate prediction of how many centuries would elapse before a combination of atmospheric cleaning and the development of the young sun would begin to melt the ice.

Of one thing Zees was sure. If any small possibility for human settlement of Worthless had ever existed, the events of the past weeks had erased that possibility for the foreseeable future.

In his imagination Goroin could see his home world covered in ice to the depth of the former height of the great scarp. It was a dismal picture, and there were times when he ceased his activity and sank into a deep depression. But there was so much to know, so much to drink in and consider.

He liked to think of the orderly system of planets which circled his sun. With that order, that astounding precision of movement, with the universe itself being such a miraculous thing and the details of planetary systems and, above all the wonder of life, how could the universe, and how could his World, allow ice to destroy all the life which had been, somehow, created?

He began to work. When he was in sole possession of that magnificent brain, then he could find a solution. Then he would rule.

There was time to consider such thoughts. He was, he knew, thinking as Moulan the Strong must think. Moulan ruled those who chose to follow him through strength, but for selfish reasons. In a way he could consider Moulan dispassionately for the first time in his life. The strong ate the weak. The strong ruled. Was that not the way of nature? If he could rule in this new body, if he proved to be the stronger, then, perhaps, it was no accident that he'd been eaten by an alien being. Perhaps it was the World's way of providing hope for the people.

If one was aged and the time had come to be eaten and one had two choices, to be eaten by a Great One or by a springer, one would choose the Great One, of course. If he had been given time to flow into his Great One he would have challenged Moulan, and he would have won. In winning he would have claimed the right of the strong, the female Great Ones, the tribute from the lesser people. And he would have awarded the newly hatched Great Ones, few in number, to his loyal followers, just as did Moulan. This was his morality.

In the mind of the human, he discovered other concepts of right and wrong. Had this human been in the body of the Great One and heard the simple observation of pure thought from Roag the Rememberer, she would not have crushed Roag underfoot. She would have discussed the concept. For there was a curious thing about these humans. Their definition of freedom extended far beyond Goroin's meaning. To him freedom meant roaming free in the desert, and not following Moulan's Rules of Order.

In a way, all the people were free. Those who served Moulan were free to leave, to join the freerunners in the desert. They chose to serve and wait and hope that one day they would be rewarded, that a newly hatched Great One would be theirs. In many ways the people were more free than any human, for, although the humans paid lip service to freedom, there was little of it, each of them bound in service to an entity called the state, and coming to blows—in war, another new concept to Goroin—in so firece a way that there now existed on the humans' home planet weapons which were capable of destroying life as surely as the coming ice would destroy life on his own world.

So what was morality? Moulan had killed. He, himself, had never killed life. The humans made no real distinction between animation and life, except to measure intelligence. To the curious human mind the death of a springer could be more painful, filled with more sadness, than the death of another human—if they were within sight of the dying springer and if they did not know the human. To Goroin, melt was an abhorrent idea, and possible extinction of real life, his people, was a horror.

He combined his musings with active searching and assaults on barriers within the human brain. Then he was distracted as all four of the humans boarded the lifeboat and, with a portable biomonitor, lowered into the swirling clouds.

"Go to the west," he kept trying to tell his host, when the party spent days on the eastern coast chasing springers. Or, as an alternative, find one of the freerunners in the desert.

New shoots were sprouting in the remnants of the eastern woodlands, and the springers were fat. The lifeboat was used to scout out life signals, and then the source of the signals was inspected.

When, at last, Don directed the lifeboat toward the western shore, Goroin's interest grew. He chuckled when the biomonitor gave life signals of a strength which astounded the humans. And he saw, through Zees' eyes, the sight which caused so much consternation in the humans.

"My God," Breed said, as the boat lowered quietly and the visuals overcame the poor visibility and four sets of eyes widened to see a group of about three dozen pocket dinosaurs performing intelligent work.

"There's the missing evolutionary link," Zees said. "Reptiles."

"They are clearing fallen trees," Ellen said incredulously.

"What I'm seeing is impossible," Don said.

"We're all dreaming," Breed said.

"It can't be that they're consciously clearing trees," Zees said. "It's a food thing or something. Perhaps there are tasty insects in the wood. Perhaps they're merely chewing off the bark."

"And to do that they're dragging the trees to form a clearing, stacking the trees," Don said.

"On Earth, things like that had a brain which was nothing much more than a spinal cord with nodes," Zees said.

Ellen was filming. "They're not big as dinosaurs go," she said. "That largest fellow, the one who is giving the orders—"

"You're making assumptions," Zees said.

"Well, he's the biggest, and he's only about twenty feet long in the body with another twenty in his tail. His head reaches up, when he stretches, about ten feet."

"Moulan," Goroin hissed, seeing the tyrant through Zees' eyes.

"Did you see that?" Ellen gasped.

The largest reptile had moved swiftly toward a struggling, smaller dino who was having trouble with a rather large tree trunk. The big one lashed out with his tail to deliver a whopping blow to the flank of the smaller. The smaller beast struggled harder and moved the tree. The big fellow went back to his point of vantage.

"That has to be intelligent behavior," Don said.

"Hey, hey," Breed said, pointing.

All of the dinosaurs had halted. A few knelt down, blowing as if tired. Others moved to nibble vegetation. Two small ones gathered mouthfuls of leaves and approached the large one, dumping the leaves in front of him. The big fellow ate. Only Goroin understood. Moulan, the leader, was having a snack served to him, as was his due.

"I'm not believing this," Zees said. "Can we land for a closer look?"

"Why not?" Don asked.

He landed a hundred yards from the clearing. He led the way through a tangle of fallen trees and underbrush until they found a wide pathway which had been cleared by pushing fallen things to one side. It was like walking through a leafy tunnel, and both men were alert, guns in hand. In each hand was enough power to kill all of the dinosaurs with one sweeping arm movement, but Don did not want to have to kill any of them. They reached the piled trees and took position to peer through and over. The dinosaurs were back at work, enlarging the clearing.

There was Moulan, so near. Goroin felt nonexistent hackles rise. Only Goroin knew how powerful were those huge legs, how swiftly they could move the huge body.

"The damned things have a social organization," Don was saying. All were suited, and the radioed talk did not escape the suits.

Yes, Goroin was thinking, it was a social organization, the only thing resembling organization on the planet. He had avoided it as Goroin Melt of Roag, for those who lived in the west were subject to the whims of Moulan.

He considered social organization for a moment. In the humans, it had begun as a family group, then expanded to the tribal level. Present human social organization served many purposes, the main one, Goroin felt, to provide the ability to pool efforts and seek a share of the resources of their planet, and to wage war. The organization of Moulan the Strong was for a different purpose. It was held together not by a need for the protection of a group, but by hope, among the lesser members, that someday they would attain Moulan's position. The smaller Great Ones wanted to mature and best Moulan and take his spoils, among them the females. The people who served the Great Ones and Goroin remained a part of the social group in the hope of earning the next Great One to be hatched from the females' fertilized eggs.

In human society the group had developed along different lines, humans combining skills to enable the group to accomplish scientific wonders, for example. From the mind of Zees he knew that the humans' planet was much older than his own. He wondered if, given time, his people would put the social group to work to discover technology. Already Moulan had discovered fire.

He was in possession of knowledge which told him that not one of the Great Ones, not even powerful Moulan, would live to see the next great invention of his people. The Great Ones, creatures of cold blood, would die with the first onslaught of the coming cold.

He felt as if he had made a discovery himself. Perhaps the World had prevented him from being eaten by his Great One, for, with Zees' knowledge, plus his own, it was apparent that nature was even before the cataclysm phasing out the Great Ones. Only one in a hundred mating rituals produced an egg. Only one in a thousand eggs hatched.

He felt a great pity for his people, especially for those in the west who followed Moulan. They were, in effect, slaves. Moulan suffered them to exist and to serve merely to breed protein food in the form of springers. Longlegs—he found himself using the human term for the people—were prolific breeders, the females producing springers in litters of as many as half a dozen.

In addition to breeding food for the Great Ones, and for themselves, the western Longlegs worked at menial tasks, gathering vegetation, clearing pathways for the Great Ones. Their numbers, of course, did not change, except, perhaps, when one tired of servitude, despaired of being selected by Moulan to be eaten by a young Great One, and took to the desert.

This brought Goroin to the most basic difference between his people and the humans. Life-force units were not subject to creation or division on his planet. Once Roag the Rememberer had undertaken the task of counting the people, and although he was not capable of covering all of the world, he arrived at an estimate of total life which, when compared to the teeming humanity on Zees' home planet, was minuscule. With his new knowledge of numbers, Goroin knew that no more than a few thousand people existed on his world.

How different it was on the other planet. There each breeding which fertilized produced another life unit. He was deep into a concept. Suppose, just suppose, that each world which created life had a measurable life force. Suppose that on the humans' Earth, that life force had been diluted by being spread among billions, while on Worthless it was concentrated in only a few thousand strong units. Then, if that theory had any validity, his force would easily overwhelm the force of this woman, Zees, if he could but find the pathways to get at it.

He retraced all he knew about the human brain, began a systematic search. He was of the people. He was strong. He would seize this body, use the human weapons to kill Moulan and free his people.

He was shocked into more self-examination by this thought. Free them? Was he being humanized?

"I'll swear that the big one tells them what to do," Zees said.

"There is purpose to their work," Don said.

The clearing was continuing. Day was coming to an end. The clearing was quite large, large enough to hold all the dinosaurs and leave room. The boss dino raised his head and roared. Work ceased. The others withdrew to the sides of the clearing.

Goroin knew what was coming, but his attention was not on Moulan. He was seeking. For the first time his host brain was being exposed to the language of his people, and he could feel the rhythm of it as if from a distance while Zees was not aware of it. Zees' brain was sensing the orders of Moulan in that area of the brain over which she had no conscious control. Goroin could feel it, almost read it, those angry, bellowed orders of the leader.

"Look, they've lined up in order of decreasing size," Ellen said.

It was true. The boss was at one end of a rough circle, and the size of the dinos graduated down away from him.

Once the Great Ones were circled, Moulan pranced to the center of the circle, orbited the clearing twice, three times, taking the nods of submission. Then he turned, raised his long neck, and bellowed. A bright glow lit the darkness. A Longlegs ran into the clearing bearing a torch, and other Longlegs followed with bundles of branches.

"My God," Zees said.

The fire was laid in the center of the clearing. Moulan watched disdainfully.

"What do you say about organized social behavior now?" Breed asked Zees.

"I say I'm astounded," Zees said truthfully.

"More company," Ellen said.

Squealing in terror, a small herd of springers were chased into the clearing by other Longlegs. The small animals leaped and scampered, trying to escape. The massed bodies of the Great Ones blocked them. The springers screamed and leaped. One leaped near Moulan. With a darting movement of his long neck Moulan seized the springer in midair. Blood sprinkled down as the tyrant chewed.

The game was to catch the springers without leaving position. The Longlegs helped, herding the panicked little animals toward the great toothed maws. Moulan ate several springers. Each of the other Great Ones was allowed only one. The remaining springers were herded away by the Longlegs.

The fire cast an eerie glow. Moulan took position in the center of the circle. He bellowed an order. The Great Ones swayed long necks, making a rhythmic hiss in unison. A dinosaur stepped forward from the circle. Goroin knew her to be female. She was in season. She was for Moulan. Goroin snarled. He heard through Zees' ears the ritual rhythm, smelled the scent of the female. She circled Moulan, her tail lifted free of the ground. Moulan was making chesty grunts.

"Fools," Goroin yelled, although he could not make himself heard.

As Longlegs he had enjoyed the freedom to blend. As a Great One he would have fought Moulan for the right, and yet his own people swayed and hissed and watched as Moulan claimed that which was the right of all.

They were his people. Each of them had had the luck to find a strong, almost indestructible body, a body which, barring accident, would live for centuries. And they meekly let Moulan claim all.

In rage, Goroin beat against the confines of his prison. And he could feel some change. He sought. He screamed. He heard the hiss and grunt of ritual from his people. He saw the organs of the males swell in empathetic excitement. He saw Moulan continue to prance, to show his great organ, to compound the degradation of his people with arrogance; and Goroin's rage sent him slashing out.

Zees moaned involuntarily as Goroin sprang, snarling, into her ego.

"The old boy is getting it on," Ellen said, as Moulan prepared for mating.

The people praised the shame. "Hail to Moulan the Great. Hail to the Father of the World."

He could hear. He was.

She could hear. She was, but she did not understand. She was hearing the people in their ritual chanting. She could smell the excitement of the female, Trinka the Lesser. When Trinka the Lesser moaned in mixed pain and joy as the Great One mounted she knew the rage of—

She felt shock. She was understanding the language of the people. Her mind was receiving communications on a nonvocal level. "Don," she said, "something funny's going on." She said it but she didn't. She could not turn her head. She felt her hand move toward her holster. She had not directed that movement. She told her hand to halt, and it did not.

And she sent. She spoke. "Hear me, people. I am Goroin Melt of Roag. I cry vengeance. I come for Moulan the Weak."

The musical language seemed to reverberate inside her. She had no control over it.

"What the hell?" Don said, as all eyes, all Great One heads, turned toward their hiding place.

"I'm going to make contact," Zees said, in her own voice.

"Zees, what the hell?"

"Leave me alone," she said. "I am in contact with them."

"Who dares?" Moulan roared, breaking off his union with Trinka the Lesser.

"Once, killer of freedom, you trod on me, melted me under your carrion-tracking foot," Goroin-Zees said. "I am Goroin Melt of Roag."

A roar of laughter came from Moulan. "Show yourself, Goroin Melt of Roag."

The people were silent, but they held position. They had not heard a challenge in many seasons. It was a challenge and it was to be honored.

"Zees, are you crazy?" Breed asked, trying to stop her.

She paused. "I told you I'm in contact with them through mental language. I have issued a challenge to their leader. We have much to learn, and to do it we must eliminate the tyrant."

"What?" Don asked. "What are you talking about."

"Watch and wait," Zees-Goroin said.

"You're going to kill the big dino?" Breed asked.

"I'm going to kill him very dead. I'm going to melt him."

"Are you sure you know what you're doing?" Don asked.

"I do. Whatever I do, don't interfere. They can't hear our radio communication. They hear only the thoughts which I direct to them."

"Come out, doomed one," Moulan was calling, as he pranced around the clearing.

She stood. There was a mass intake of breath from the Great Ones. The female who had had her moment broken looked at the newcomer with hate, wanting Moulan to crush and kill quickly.

"I know not the form," Moulan said. Was there, Goroin thought smugly, just a tiny bit of fear in his voice? "But it should crush as easily as did Roag the Foolish. Come down, small one. Come and feel the wrath of Moulan."

Zees could not determine what had happened to her. She seemed to exist in two planes, a true Gemini. She felt herself leap lightly to the packed earth of the clearing. She was a participant and yet she had no control of her actions. She knew the joy, the anger of Goroin Melt of Roag. She knew his memories. It was there and only the excitement of the moment saved her from the trauma of suddenly being two.

Goroin, once he had the key, had dominated her easily. He was the strong one. His were the actions, his the body.

He moved forward. Moulan was prancing ceremoniously, moving backward and forth, stomping his huge feet, weaving his neck in complicated patterns.

There was time. "Fear not, woman of Earth called Zees," Goroin said.

"I hear you," Zees said. She did not speak aloud, could not. "Who are you?"

"We will talk," Goroin said. Never had two life units existed in the same brain without madness. "Later."

"Must we—must you kill him?" Zees asked.

"Look into my memories."

"I have."

"Then you see."

"You must, I suppose."

"Do you feel fear, Moulan the Coward?" Goroin asked.

"Does the small one talk or challenge?" Moulan retorted.

"Look, Moulan. Look and know fear." He blasted the top from a nearby tree. The vegetation glowed and burst into flame. The top of the tree fell, shattering brush underneath it.

The Great Ones let out a mass sigh, a hiss of fear.

"Not you, my people," Goroin said. "Fear is only for the tyrant."

He saw Moulan's legs go tense, bunch themselves for a rush. He knew the speed of which Moulan was capable, and he knew that the human body would crush as easily as that of Roag, as Moulan had said. Moulan reared and gave a showy trumpet of anger. For a moment the people thought that it would be over soon, that the challenger would be crushed as, so long ago, Roag the Rememberer had been crushed.

Goroin blasted away the two front legs which were raised to smash him. He stepped aside. Moulan, screaming in shock and pain, fell to the ground, thudding the bloody stumps of his legs against the packed earth.

But Moulan was a fighter. He lashed with his tail, swiveling his body to deliver a potentially deadly blow. The tail disintegrated in a spatter of blood and flesh. Mutilated, bleeding, Moulan let his forward body sag to the ground.

"Now you will melt," Goroin said. "You will melt as Roag melted. You will be food for the people, then carrion for the scavengers, but long before we feast on the flesh which was yours, you, yourself, will be in nothingness, there to be absorbed by the first small passing animal. I will see to it that it is a food creature."

Moulan roared hate, reared on his intact rear legs, lunged from his maximum height. He darted his powerful neck down, whiplashing the heavy head to strike down the one who had destroyed him. He lost his rear legs then, and was a limbless, bloodless torso with his body rolling onto its side. He lifted his head, knowing pain and the beginnings of fear.

"He has the power of the southern fires," moaned Trinka the Lesser. "He is great."

"Hail Goroin Melt of Roag," called out a male, bowing.

"Silence," Goroin thundered. "Bow to no one except in mutual respect."

He turned to the fallen Moulan. "Moulan the dead," he said. "Say your farewells, for now you melt."

"You have won, oh Great Goroin," Moulan said, in agony. "Have mercy."

"As you had mercy on Roag?"

"In the breeding pens there is a small and insignificant Great One," Moulan said. "Could that body be mine you will not regret your mercy."

"Eh? Would we rule together, Moulan?" Goroin asked. He laughed. The sound seemed to drive the last hope from Moulan's clouding eyes.

"Must you melt him?" Zees asked.

"You know my memories. His life unit must be cleansed of past excesses."

"Would not transformation into a springer be cleansing?"

"I, Moulan, once Strong, beg of you," the fallen leader said, his force growing weaker. "A springer, Great Goroin. A springer only. Let me know that much, at least. I could do you, who hold the power of the fires, no harm."

The people were hushed. Moulan's life's blood continued to pour.

"Did I not gather the people?" Moulan asked. "Did I not

take them from their solitary ways and unite them in great and noble efforts?''

"But you led badly," Goroin said. "Where are the others? Where are the many Great Ones?"

"The earthpains," Moulan groaned. "Many were near the sea, living in plenty. They sank when the sea came to them. Others were crushed. Many melted. We are all that is left, Great Goroin. We are so few. We have emptied many life units, which now float to, perhaps, rejoin us someday. They will need training. There are many newly eaten people who are but springers.''

"He is right, Great Goroin," said the bold Trinka the Lesser. "We are few."

"Don't waste him, Goroin," said Zees. "His mind is old and contains much, things that not even you know about the people."

"Yes," Goroin Melt of Roag said. He circled the body of the fallen leader. "I will show mercy. I will set an example for the people. But hear this. Tyranny is no more. We are a people, be we man or Great One. We will work together. We face problems of which none of you is yet aware. With these problems we will have the help of friends from a far place—"

"Goroin, don't build false hopes," Zees said.

"Silence, woman who is known as Zees," he said to her internally. And, to the people, "Bring him then, a healthy springer. We will forgive. We will welcome him among us in his natural form."

To the humans: "Hey, it's almost over. Hang in there and I'll introduce you to my new friends."

Don and the others watched in wonder as a frogroo was brought in and placed on the ground beside Moulan's bloody ruin. The springer had been without food for days, and was ready.

"Trinka the Lesser," said Goroin, "you will prepare him."

Moulan was weakening rapidly. Trinka the Lesser swept her sharp teeth through the tender belly, lanced the hide and exposed internal organs. Moulan flowed into the soft and tasty liver and passed over as the hungry springer attacked the still-pulsing organ.

Moulan the Repentant strengthened his new body with the repast and drank of the flowing blood.

Finished, Moulan turned. "Hail, Great Goroin."

"My people," Goroin said, "we will not waste. There is a feast for all."

"Hail Great Goroin," they chanted.

"Before we feast," Goroin said, "we will honor our guests."

"Don," Zees-Goroin said, "bring everyone out."

Goroin did not have all the answers, but he was planning far ahead. He had no trouble, once having found the way, in controlling the body of Zees. Through her he could influence the others. And they, the humans, had to eat sometime.

The people hissed in surprise as the three beings identical to the Great Goroin entered the clearing.

"How can you talk to these things?" Ellen asked.

"You've got some explaining to do," Breed said. "What are you, the big bwana around here now that you've killed the leader?"

"I am Goroin Melt of Roag," he said. "I am the new leader of the people. Henceforth I am to be known as Goroin the Deliverer."

"Congratulations," Don said. "Now what?"

"We are invited to dine," Zees-Goroin said. "We waste not on this poor world. We feast on the body of the fallen tyrant, Moulan."

"Dinosaur steak," Ellen said. "Well, it's different."

"You'll find it to be delicious," Zees said. "We will call the—" He almost used the other word which translated into a word quite familiar to the humans. "We will call the Longlegs to prepare our food, to cook it over an open fire."

Trinka the Lesser supervised the butchering of the body of him who was almost the sire of her seeded eggs. The Longlegs aided. Three Longlegs showed tender cuts to the humans. Zees-Goroin nodded approval. The cooking meat smelled delicious in the open air.

Don, Breed and Ellen were full of questions.

"They call themselves the people," Zees-Goroin explained. "They consider themselves to be one."

"But intelligent dinosaurs?" Breed asked.

"Their, ah, intelligence is equal to and no greater than the intelligence of the Longlegs," he explained.

"The frogroos are not intelligent?"

"Only animate," he said. "Those animals are called spring-ers, for the way they are always springing about."

"How do you speak?" Don asked.

"I think I can explain that better later," he said. "I think, in fact, that it can be taught." He thought for a moment. "It just came to me. I felt this sort of tickling sensation in my brain and suddenly there it was, I was open. Their language is strictly mental."

"What do they call themselves?" Ellen asked.

He mused for a moment. "You realize that it's difficult to translate from a language without words to an oral language."

"I can understand that," Don said.

"The dinos are called Great Ones. The Longlegs are called men."

"Well, that figures," Don said. "And I suppose the name for their planet translates to be Earth."

"Yes," he said. "With a capital letter, the World, as a sort of nondivine thing to be prayed to, or wished to. But in general, yes, they call Worthless the Earth."

"If they had a spoken language," Ellen said, "the sound of the name would be different, but it would come out meaning the same thing, Earth."

Around them the people were feasting, Great Ones and the rather nervous-looking Longlegs, not really at ease to be eating in the presence of the ruling class.

"Tell the Men of the Earth," said Don, "that the Men of the Earth from far away appreciate their hospitality."

"Yes, it has been done," Zees-Goroin said.

"Zees," Ellen said, "tell me more about how you first sensed the mental communication."

"It's difficult to explain," Zees-Goroin said. "Let me think about it for a while. In the meantime, we've got prob-lems. We've met an intelligent alien people and unless we do something they're going to become extinct. The dinos can't last through the first severe winter. The Longlegs are more adaptable, but they can't weather an ice age."

"Zees, I know how you feel," Don said. "But what can

we do? We've got problems of our own. Every day we spend here is one day we could be using trying to accomplish our primary mission.''

"We can't just abandon them," Zees-Goroin said. He had no intention of abandoning them.

"Zees, when it comes to making a choice between looking after the welfare of our own people and that of these people, what choice is there?" Ellen asked.

None, he thought. None at all. If the people of that distant Earth chose to destroy themselves by overcrowding, well, there were others to help. There were two more ships in deep space looking for lifezone planets, and the far Earth had the technical capacity to build transporters should livable planets be found. Poor Worthless had nothing. Worthless had one hope, and it was in the form of four humans.

",Damn, I'd like to be able to talk with them," Breed said, as he watched two Longlegs bow politely to each other and share a piece of flesh.

"I think I know a way," Zees-Goroin said. Yes, he knew. It was merely a matter of finding the right person to take over Breed's body. Then two more for the others.

11

FOR three days Zees-Goroin acted as translator. He was still undecided, in fact, more and more doubtful of giving power equal to his to any of his people. There seemed to be, in all of the remnants of the once-numerous group which had been led by Moulan, only one who had a mind of her own. Trinka the Lesser, the female in the body of a great and mature beast. She became his good right hand as he tried to instill in the people a new sense of freedom. They were not yet ready to be told that their world was beginning a change which would doom them.

The fascination of learning from an alien intelligence held the attention of Breed, Ellen and Don. Zees-Goroin saw to it that information was parceled out in intriguing doses, just enough to hold interest.

Zees, a prisoner inside her own being, knowing all, was even more fascinated. She had come to sense a basic goodness in the being which dominated her, and held long conversations with him.

Goroin was not in favor of anyone's returning, just yet, to the orbiting *Santa Maria*, but Zees knew the necessity—one just doesn't leave machinery unsupervised for too long, not when that machinery is one's only link with home and, in Goroin's case, with hope. She convinced Don to stay with her. Don took Breed and Ellen up to the ship and returned in the lifeboat.

It was discouraging to Goroin to see the depths of dependence to which his people had sunk under the rule of Moulan. It was a bit frightening to know that the strongest mind among them was that of Moulan himself, now growing a springer. He was still Moulan the Strong. His knowledge was great, and there was even a temptation to allow Moulan to join him in control of a human body. But he dared not. There was a dark side to Moulan, and he was more than ever convinced that Roag had been right, Moulan had once been eaten into double occupancy and had undergone the terrible madness.

He found in the people nothing but sloth and servility. Great Ones who could have snuffed out his life with the mighty stomp of one foot bowed and called him the Great Goroin. Longlegs came to him with gifts of tender edibles. Each of them bowed, begged, prostrated himself, thinking in the old ways, still foolishly wishing for the ultimate fulfillment, the body of a Great One, not knowing that the Great Ones would be the first to die in the coming cold. The rule of Moulan had left scars.

There was, however, a possible answer to his dilemma. Out in the vastness of the desert were the free roamers. Their minds had not known the tyranny of Moulan, or, had they experienced it, they had fled it. Their thinking would be free, free as the space which they roamed. And among them, if the World pleased, would be one whom he could trust implicitly. Among the free roamers was Melin of Grace. He knew that splendid mind, knew it to be willful and untouched by fear. Melin, if she had survived the cataclysm, would work with him and together they would find two others of free and independent spirit.

Goroin issued orders to his people. They were accustomed to taking orders. "You will fashion tools, thus," he said, using the knowledge of human anthropology to find flintlike rock, fashion it. "You will hew the tall trees into logs, thus," he said, demonstrating.

"Log cabins?" Don asked. "They'll merely postpone the inevitable."

"It will give them some time," Zees said.

"It is little enough, I suppose," Don agreed. He pitched in with a will.

"I want to see how the people of the desert came through the cataclysm," Zees said. Don agreed. Goroin left the larg-

est of the Great Ones, Pudee the Helper, in charge. The
people were content. They had work. They had food. They
had a strong leader.

Zees-Goroin stalled Don's continuing efforts to sense the
mental communication by giving him meaningless mental
exercises to do.

Don Duckworth was a man of action, and he was more
than ready to move. He had set a deadline in his mind. He
would give Zees a month, no more, to help prepare the
Longlegs for the eternal winter which awaited them. Then he
would lift ship and move. In the meantime, he was happy to
leave the western area and explore the desert.

Goroin, in spite of the sad knowledge of doom which he
carried, felt a lifting of spirits as the lifeboat flew low over
the vast desert. He found free roamers. He talked with them
and kept Don's interest high with translated tales of their
attitudes and travels. He was refreshed by their fierce
independence.

He found an old one who was near death. The old one
asked, since Goroin could fly, had he seen any free-roaming
Great Ones. Goroin sadly said no. He suggested that the old
one find a springer.

"Do as I tell you, old one," he said, "and soon I will find
you, in your new youth, and bring great hope." For he was
impressed with the old one, with Ords the Freerunner. It was
a mind which he could admire.

He knew the greatest joy he'd known since seeing his own
Great One when he sensed the presence of Melin of Grace.
So strong was her mind that he felt it from on high and sent
the ship down, down, then slowed, so as not to startle her.

She stood with her head high, nose pointed upward, watching the slow lowering of the strange thing. She was not
afraid. Goroin felt himself quiver with her beauty. She was
near what had been their favorite watering place, a tiny spring
which was known by few, nothing more than a slow drip
from a facade of stone. She was sleek and well fed.

"Melin, Melin," he sent. "Be not afraid, it is I."

"Goroin," she said joyfully. "But you are, indeed, strange."

"More strange than you can imagine," he said.

"You fly."

"Yes, but the thing you see is not Goroin."

"Then where is Goroin?" She awaited as he landed the ship. When he stepped out she approached, long, beautiful ears thrust forward.

"You have wonderful powers," she said. "And yet when you left me you went in search of a Great One."

"What is he saying?" Don asked.

"It is a female," Zees-Goroin told him. "She welcomes us to her range."

Don followed Zees-Goroin's example, bowed, touching his hands to the earth. Goroin was telling all, in swift bursts of information, pleased with Melin's lack of questions and her understanding. Her great, free mind was absorbing all, even the strange idea of creatures not of her earth, for she was seeing with her own eyes. Her Goroin had returned, as he had promised. He had, as he had promised, revenged the melt of Roag the Rememberer. Now he had achieved greatness.

"World, Melin, how I've missed you," he said.

"How can we be together with you in such form?" she asked.

"In the bodies of these humans," he said.

She laughed. "You are female."

"And you will be male," he said, equally amused by the idea. "You must have absolute faith in me. Tonight, when the male sleeps, you will transform into the body of a food creature."

"If that is the way," she said doubtfully.

"It is the way," he said.

"This one is interesting," Zees-Goroin said to Don. "She was in the south when the cataclysm came."

"You're lying," Zees told him.

"It is the only way, woman," he told her.

"It is not right," she said. "You have taken me, Goroin. It is wrong to take another being."

"It is wrong to see my world die," he said.

"We could help more as free people," she said. "I have heard you speak to your people. I have heard you tell them about freedom, and yet you do as Moulan once did, you dominate me. You deprive me of my freedom."

"I am saddened," Goroin said truthfully. "I see no other way."

"That's because you're trying to solve it all yourself," she said. "Allow us to help."

"I will have your help," he said.

"Melin of Grace asks that we stay and talk with her," he told Don.

It was growing late. Don set up the portatents from the lifeboat. As he worked, Goroin and Melin had a few delicious moments alone, minutes which they spent in wonderful wastefulness, remembering how the sun felt on the first day of their meeting, speaking of their first blending.

Melin, after the group had talked until darkness fell, curled up by the spring and pretended sleep. When Don was sleeping soundly, Zees-Goroin and Melin left the camp, sought out a small food creature which was stunned by the human weapon. When the animal revived, held in Zees' gloved hands, it was not inclined to eat. However, Goroin the Deliverer was no longer bound by traditional ways. He shaved a spot under Melin's arm to expose tender flesh. He directed Melin to flow into the exposed areas, then, using the suit's medical kit, lanced the shaved area to cause a flow of blood. He held the food creature's mouth open until it was filled with blood and with Melin of Grace and then forced the animal to swallow, by holding its nose and forcing the mouth closed.

"I am small and helpless," Melin said, in her new body.

The undamaged Longlegs, devoid of life, returned to the animation of the springer, hopped away.

"You will not be thus long," Goroin said.

In the dim dawn Goroin woke Duckworth. "Our friend seems to have left us," he told Don. "I awoke early and went to look for her. While I was walking I got breakfast."

"Good," Don said. "Whose turn to be cook?"

"If you'll start a fire I'll do the honors."

Don started a fire. A desert plant, thick and tough, made good firewood.

"I will make it as painless as I can," Goroin told Melin. Melin was, in the body of the food creature, feigning death. She almost winced, however, as Goroin skinned a rear leg. She flowed at his instructions.

"Remember when we ate it raw?" Zees-Goroin asked.

"Not too bad, as I remember," Don said.

Zees-Goroin took a bite from the exposed flesh. 'Humm,'' she said. She extended it. "Try it?"

"I'll take mine medium," he said.

"I must be reverting to primitivism," Zees-Goroin said. "It's good."

Don gave it a try, but not with much enthusiasm. He took a small bite, tearing it away with his teeth. Melin flowed. She had been prepared for the moment. She knew in advance what Goroin had taken days to discover. She took only a few moments to adjust, then assaulted the barrier immediately.

It was quick.

"I am," Melin said.

"Rest," Goroin told her. "Absorb." He fed. He passed raw flesh to Don-Melin, who chewed thoughtfully.

"He takes it well," Melin said.

Don was recovering from his initial shock. "Zees, are you like this?" he asked, but his words did not leave his captive mind.

"She is thus," Melin said. "Fear not. She is unharmed."

Goroin gave Melin time. They finished their meal in a leisurely fashion. He could feel Melin's growing excitement as she knew the full potential of power which she now possessed, as she was exposed to the knowledge in Don's mind. Their talk was the talk of the people, mind to mind, and it was shared by Zees and Don Duckworth.

To know her new body better, Melin removed the heavy suit. She quickly discovered that she had to keep filters over her breathing apparatus.

"I am thinking of Ords the Freerunner as an ally," Goroin said.

"I have talked with him," Melin said. "I agree."

"That leaves but one," Goroin said.

"There is another," she said. "We have hunted together. I know her range."

"Good," he said.

They boarded the lifeboat. The thoughts which were coming from Melin's mind were intriguing.

"Yes," Goroin said. "These bodies have a great capacity for pleasure."

"We must know all about our bodies," Melin said, with overtones of suggestion.

"That is logical," Goroin said.

The sleep accommodations of the lifeboat were quite large enough for the experiment.

12

ONE of the primary requirements for space duty was a stable personality. Don Duckworth was one of the best-adjusted men ever to take qualification tests. When he found himself imprisoned inside his own brain, his body dominated by an alien, he did not scream and flail about. He recognized the situation and began to consider it a problem, a very unique problem, to be solved.

He was aware of the lovemaking and enjoyed it, found sensations heightened by the joy felt by Melin and Goroin at being together again. Because of their preoccupation, he was left quite alone and given time to adjust. He soon realized that he was cut off completely from Zees, but that he had contact with Melin.

After the pleasurable interlude ended and the two bodies lay entwined, he spoke. "Melin of Grace, Goroin's plan will merely delay the inevitable."

"And yet it is better than nothing," she said.

"By keeping us, you prevent us from doing our duty to our people," Don said.

"We, too, have a duty."

"Taking control of the others will not be necessary," Don said. "They will help. You and Goroin are close. You can trust each other. But how can you be sure of others?"

"I will follow Goroin," she said simply.

"Is it not true that if you flowed back into a Longlegs you would retain my knowledge?" he asked. "Then we would be Men together, not captor and prisoner."

"Then we would not have your weapons. We would be at your mercy," she said.

"Among friends weapons are not necessary," Don said. "We are all creatures of the universe. We live in worlds which were formed by nature. We share intelligent life."

Melin opened the conversation, shared it with Goroin.

"Our people face the more immediate danger," he said.

"Goroin, can you, through Melin, look into my mind?" Don asked.

"I have seen all in the mind of Zees," Goroin said.

"But Zees sees things in a different light," Don said.

"I can read you," Goroin said.

He looked. He saw warships. He saw armaments which could destroy his world.

"But I know this," Goroin said. "I know that you kill your fellow creatures."

"Yes," Don said. "But consider this. We have never had an alien enemy." He did not have to communicate it, for Goroin had seen, and had been startled, but he continued, and Goroin allowed it to give himself time to think. "One reason Breed and Ellen went back to the ship was to put through a long-delayed message to our planet."

Goroin understood. Even now the message was blinking outward. And the far planet would know that the *Santa Maria* had encountered intelligent alien life. And Goroin saw, in Don's mind, a facet of humanity which he had not encountered, xenophobia.

"We know you are not a monster," Don said. "But think how others might feel, knowing that your people have the power to take over the human body, to dominate the mind. Look into my mind and see the result."

Huge ships, heavily armed. Men with death-dealing weapons coming to wipe out the monsters.

"Your Earth is far away. There are problems there. Your people are intent on destroying themselves."

"But men will come," Don said. "When our message is received and we do not make contact again, if we do not return at the expected time, men will come to see if the intelligent life which we reported had something to do with our disappearance. Your world has been revealed to them

They will, all of them, turn on you as the enemy.''

"It would give us more human bodies to occupy," Melin said.

"A thousand men? Any one of which, discovering the truth, could destroy you?''

Goroin was silent.

"As friends, we can help," Don said. "Quite frankly, not all the knowledge of Earth can prevent the ice age from coming.''

"In your bodies, we will ask for aid in moving our people to another place," Goroin said.

"We know of only one other lifezone planet," Don said. "Our Earth.''

"Goroin," Zees said. "I know you. I have shared many days with you. You are a gentle being. Did you not spare Moulan? I know your hopes, your fears. I share them with you. Give us the opportunity to work with you and we will help willingly and accomplish much which you cannot.''

"I control," Goroin said.

"You have formed your plans without the willing and conscious aid of Zees, of myself," Don said. "You have our knowledge, but it is new to you. Perhaps you cannot use it as well as we could use it together.''

"The man called Don has good intentions," Melin said. "I can sense them.''

"We can and will help in any way possible," Don said.

"In return for what?" Goroin said.

"Ourselves," Don said.

Zees was thinking furiously.

"I cannot agree to that," Goroin said.

"I understand," Zees told him. "But consider this, Goroin. Don has touched on something which had not occurred to me. On our planet people vie with each other. There simply are not enough resources to go around. It seems quite likely, if we do not find lifezone planets soon, and give hope to Earth for relief from hunger and want, that the mad ones among us will fight, and then all will be destroyed. But what if we show them that there are others, whose problems are more immediate? If we show our people that they are not alone in the universe, that at least one other intelligent race exists, and is in desperate need of help, perhaps that will be a unifying factor. Perhaps our two races can then work together."

"Yes," Don said eagerly. "The simple fact that your planet exists, that conditions for life came about on a world other than Earth, will give new hope. We could concentrate all our resources on new exploration ships. Together we could find new homes for all, for your people and for ours."

"Goroin, there is time before the ice comes," Zees said.

"Even now it forms at the poles," Goroin said.

"But there is time," Don insisted.

"There is also time before your Earth sends warships," Goroin said. "And no assurance that your promises of help would be kept by your people." He shook his human head.

"No," Goroin said. "For the moment we will do as I had planned. We need your tools, your weapons. The cold will begin. We must have shelter. We can't do it with stone weapons."

"There is this, too, Goroin," Zees said. "I have been with you for some time now. I have studied and probed. You, upon entering, came into this part of my brain." She knew he was aware of the area. "You did not understand why it was so little utilized."

"You are right," he said.

"In time, I can use the power of this portion of my brain to displace you," Zees said. "Thus." She pushed. Goroin, startled, felt himself shrink and shift, and it was with effort that he maintained control.

"That way lies madness," he warned, fear very real in him.

"Perhaps," Zees said. "But am I given a choice?"

"I beg you not to try," Goroin said. "See in my memories the maddened carnivore of Roag the Rememberer."

"We should not battle," Zees said. "But I will fight, Goroin. I promise you that I will do all within my power to regain what is mine."

"So be it," he said. "Perhaps, before you lose us both in insanity, we can accomplish some good."

The Longlegs abandoned by Melin of Grace had not wandered far. It was grazing peacefully and offered no resistance. With the Longlegs inside the lifeboat they located Ords the

Freerunner. He, suspicious of such a fine body unoccupied, examined the Longlegs closely before allowing himself to be eaten.

Mank the Soft, Melin's hunting companion, was located in her usual range. When she was told that Moulan was no longer ruler, that the World faced danger, she accompanied them. In the west the people had dawdled. Not one log cabin was complete.

Angered, Goroin called the people together and spoke to them. He demonstrated the power of weapons by flaming a tree, and ordered the work to go forward.

"Now we will call down the others," he said.

"It's about time you got in touch," Breed said, when Melin-Don called the *Maria*. "Something's hit the fan back home, Don. We took a blink message with orders to head for home soonest, direct, and to identify quickly when we're in range."

"Any idea what's happening?" Melin-Don asked.

"War," Don told her.

"The order is urgent and imperative," Breed said. "My guess is they want to mount guns on the *Maria*."

"Breed," Don-Melin said. "You and Ellen get ready. I'll send Zees up in the boat and get you and we'll talk this over."

"Don, we've got orders," Breed said. "You're the captain, but I'd suggest you two get up here. I'm building power now. We'll be ready to blink by the time you get here."

"Goroin, you must let us go," Zees said. "We'll tell them about you. We'll try to send help."

Goroin could not think fast enough. "I'll send the boat up," Don-Melin repeated. "You two come on down."

"They won't come," Zees said. "You don't know us as well as you thought, Goroin. You've made Breed suspicious. He knows that Don wouldn't disobey a direct order."

"We will overpower them on board the ship," Goroin said, "and force them to eat."

13

"CURIOUS," Breed said, as he broke the connection with the lifeboat.

"I'll agree that it is not at all like Don," Ellen said.

"I can understand how Zees got caught up in the plight of the Longlegs," Breed said. "I can feel for the poor bastards myself. They're interesting people, and with a little time they could go far. But there's nothing we can do. It's just rather tragic that they developed so early in the life cycle of their sun. They'll be wiped out, sure as anything. But we're helpless. And we've got orders."

Ellen had felt physically ill when she read the order which had been sent so many light-years by the blink beacons which *Maria* had planted on the way out. After over two years with her nice little family on board ship it was hard to believe that those idiots back on Earth were squaring off to fight yet another war, perhaps, if the madmen pushed the right buttons, the last war.

"I've got half a notion to stay right here," she said. "I think I'd rather help the Longlegs fight nature than go home and fight people."

"Yeah, I know how you feel," Breed said. "Maybe it's not war. Maybe one of the other ships found better pickings than we. Maybe the *Nina* or the *Pinta* hit paydirt and found a sector thick with lifezone planets and they need us for exploration."

"I wish I could think you are right," Ellen said.

"What's with Don? What's this you two come down and we'll talk stuff?" Breed asked.

"Oh, I imagine he's just getting emotionally involved with the situation down there," she said.

"As a doctor, Ellen, what's your opinion on the way Zees has been acting?"

"How do you mean?" she said. "If you're thinking of the ease with which she established mental contact, I'm wondering about that myself. I have no idea how it's done. Her explanations didn't make much sense."

"I used to play around with extrasensory perception," Breed said. "I was pretty sensitive. It seems to be a characteristic of the American Indian. I was a whiz at guessing games and I could defy the odds, and try as I might I could never get one communication via telepathy. It just seems funny that Zees, the practical one, should get the signals from a species which communicates by telepathy."

"What's bothering you?" Ellen asked.

"Don Duckworth is a serviceman. He's been in space service almost fifty years. You know it and I know it. He's easy to get along with, but when it comes to regulations he goes by the book."

"Yes, I see what you mean," Ellen said.

"It's just not like him to ignore a direct order," Breed said. "Something is very, very wrong."

"What could be wrong?" She laughed. "You sound as if you might believe he's being held hostage by the aliens."

He laughed. "Make a great thriller. I was held captive by dinosaurs."

The radio came to life. "Hey, Breed," Don's voice said. "We're coming up."

Breed looked at Ellen. She went to the radio. "Hi, Don. Have you lifted off?"

"Sure thing," he said. "In fact, we're about ten minutes out. Put a candle in the window, mother, and open the ship's bay."

"Will do," Ellen said. She looked at Breed questioningly.

He leaned close and spoke. "Don, I've got almost full power on the generators. I've fed the blink coordinates into the computer and we can skip two beacons on the first jump home."

"Ah, roger on that," Don said. "OK, we've got you visual."

Breed flipped monitor switches. "Got you, Don. Stand by to go automatic."

"Roger," Don said.

Breed pushed buttons and the shipboard computer took control of the lifeboat, wafting it swiftly toward the *Maria*. Down below air hissed out of the boat bay to be stored. The outer doors opened.

He heard a series of clicks, saw lights flash. He checked. "Strange," he said. "The boat's about three hundred pounds heavy."

"I guess they're bringing artifacts," Ellen said.

"What artifacts?" Breed asked, his fingers flying. He activated the biomonitor, focused it close. The signals from the lifeboat were unmistakable. "Ellen, they have two Long-legs with them," he said.

She looked at him in puzzlement, started to open the mike to talk with the boat. Breed put his hand on hers. "No, hold it," he said.

He could feel the slight clank of metal as the lifeboat settled in the bay. He felt a bit silly, questioning the acts of his captain, a man he'd come to respect and like, but he'd always been a doubter. He believed in the ancient principles which are constantly at work to louse up any well-made plan. If something can go wrong it will.

"Ellen, you take over," he said. "Give me about three minutes before you let the air back into the bay." He was reaching for his suit, his weapons.

"Breed, you're scaring me," Ellen said in protest.

"Just caution, baby," he said. "Give them air three minutes from now, OK?"

"Three minutes," she said.

"Put on that headset and set it for channel 30," he told her. She obeyed. A quick check showed his suit radio to be working. He ran back toward the stern and the boat bay.

"Air going in," Ellen said, on the channel which was not used too often, a channel not likely to be monitored by Don and Zees.

He hid in an equipment closet in the corridor outside the

boat bay, door slightly ajar. He could hear the air hissing into the bay and then the clang as the lock was released. He waited. The hatch to the bay opened. Don was the first one to come out. He was flipping up his visor and it was just old Don, but there was grimness on his face and behind him a silent Zees. They paused, looked around. They did not speak, but each reached for his weapon at the same time, lifted it, dialed it to a stun charge large enough to stop a man. Breed was holding his breath. Zees and Don moved up the corridor, and Breed waited, expecting to see the Longlegs emerge from the bay. When they did not, and when his two shipmates were out of sight, he slipped across the corridor. He peered cautiously into the boat bay and saw movement.

At first Mank the Soft thought that Melin-Don had returned. She stepped from behind the liftboat and asked what was wrong. Ords the Freerunner followed. The stun blast from Breed's weapon caught them together, fanned over them, and Mank felt herself falling without pain but with no feeling, no ability to move.

"Ellen," Breed radioed, "leave the bridge immediately. Take the galley passageway."

Ellen obeyed, impressed by the urgency in Breed's voice.

Goroin-Zees pushed open the door to the bridge with his left hand, his right holding his weapon, set on stun. He leaped in. The room was empty.

"Goroin," Zees told him, "give it up. They know."

"There is no way they can know. They cannot even suspect," Goroin said, but Zees could feel his doubt. She knew his discomfort. In possession of her knowledge as he was, he was still aboard an alien ship. He had adjusted to the new ocean of knowledge in the human brain with amazing swiftness, but he was still at a disadvantage, for the knowledge had been a part of him for only a short time. The weapon in his hand was as effective as the one which Breed held, as he padded softly up the corridor toward the bridge, but Goroin had never used it.

Breed paused at an off-bridge monitor station and flipped switches. The scene on the bridge confirmed his suspicions that something was very wrong. His captain and his friend, Zees, stood there uncertainly with weapons in their hands.

"Breed, Ellen," Melin-Don called, "where are you?"

Breed punched buttons to open a repair port, entered the inner hull, took position at a vent looking into the bridge area. He adjusted his radio to the frequency of the radios in the suits.

"Don, Zees, put down the weapons," he said softly. "Put them down now."

Goroin went stiff. "Where is he?" he asked Zees. Then he knew, saw it in her mind, whirled to aim his weapon toward the vent. The stun force sprayed out and was dissipated by metal. It was all the proof that Breed needed. The muzzle of his weapon was thrust through a small slit in the vent.

Zees felt the force hit her, felt Goroin lose his control. She felt her body falling and in the time that it took to fall, she was busy. She had been awaiting such a moment. She had been gathering force and she used it, assaulting Goroin with all the strength she had as he, in confusion, was helpless. For a moment it seemed that he was right in predicting madness, for there was madness in the struggle until, with a scream of frustration, Goroin was banished. Once again he was imprisoned, helpless, and his struggles were useless.

"No, no," Zees told him. "Don't struggle so. It will be all right. I promise you."

She knew that the stun charge would keep her body immobile for almost a quarter hour and then begin to wear off gradually. She could not even move her eyes, but she was not the same Zees that she had been before an alien intelligence, a strange and inexplicable life force, had taken domination of her very brain and body. She explored. Yes, it was there. By having been thrust back, back, deep inside that little-known area of her brain where the subconscious dwelt, where dreams were formed, an area of vast underutilization, she had learned, and there was a power there which astounded her, for although she could not move her eyes she could see, could sense it as Breed entered the control bridge carefully, weapon at the ready.

She could not feel as Breed and Ellen used restrainers to bind her arms and her legs, but she knew. And she knew their puzzled thoughts and wanted to weep for Breed, in his sadness. He had blasted two of his family. He did not understand what was happening.

"Darling Breed," she said, "it's all right."

He went stiff, looked around. "Did you hear that?" he asked Ellen.

"Don't worry," Zees said to both of them. "Everything will be all right now."

"Zees?" Ellen asked in wonder, bending to lift one of Zees limp eyelids. "It's impossible," she said to Breed. "She's out."

"Only my body," Zees said. "I'm here."

"Good God," Breed said, moving back, holding his weapon ready. He was looking around wildly. "Where are you, Zees? What's happened to you?"

"Put away the weapons, kiddies," Zees said. "I can explain."

"I'm not believing this," Ellen said.

"Ellen, please see to the Longlegs," Zees said. "The charge you used on them was strong. They'll need help."

Ellen looked at Breed doubtfully. "Go take a look," he said.

"Give them only a half dose of reviver," Zees said.

"Don't let them melt," Goroin begged. He had accepted the new status. He was still a part of Zees, and he was impressed. He could feel the power. He could see possibilities that Zees herself, so newly back in control, had not seen. He was awed. He knew that he would never again be able to dominate her.

"No, we won't," Zees said.

She watched as Ellen ran to the bay and checked the vital signs of the two Longlegs. As Zees had indicated, the charge had been nearly lethal. The involuntary functions of life had been partially halted and the two Longlegs were breathing with a weak, erratic rhythm. She broke open syringes and injected each of them with half a dose of the reviver. The labored breathing eased almost immediately.

"They'll be out for a while," Zees said, speaking to her there in the bay as she'd spoken on the control bridge, and Ellen felt new fear. She clasped her hands to her ears and tried to close them.

"Yes," Zees said. "You're not hearing me with your ears, Ellen."

Ellen ran back. Breed was standing uncertainly, weapon still aimed at the two on the deck.

"Breed, I have feeling coming back into my fingers and toes," Zees said. "When I can, I'm going to sit up very slowly. No sudden movements. All right?"

"You're not hearing her with your ears," Ellen told him.

"I've just realized that," Breed said. "All right, Zees. We'll be watching you very closely."

She was able to accelerate the process. Don's body was still limp when she sat up very slowly and opened her eyes. She smiled up at Breed and Ellen.

"Kiddies," she said, "you're going to have one helluva time believing what happened."

It seemed to be Zees. The smile was Zees'. The eyes were Zees', and she was now speaking.

"You saved the situation, Breed, by knowing Don so well," Zees said. "By knowing that he would not question a direct order."

"The aliens?" Breed asked. "Were those two in the bay controlling you in some way?" No, he thought quickly, that was not it, for they had continued to brandish weapons after he'd stunned the Longlegs in the bay.

"Not those two," Zees said. She tapped her head. "I have a guest. Up here."

Breed lifted his weapon quickly. "Easy," Zees said. "I've regained control. And the natives are friendly. They mean no real harm. They're just concerned about the fate of their world. They wanted our help, and they thought they could get it best by seizing control."

"How do we know they're not still in control?" Ellen asked.

"That's a problem," Zees admitted. "I think it's going to take an act of faith on your part to show you exactly what the situation is. Why don't you give Don a blast of reviver, Ellen. Then I'll be able to show you something."

Ellen took the suggestion. Soon Don began to stir. He sat up with a jerk, and Breed's weapon was on him.

"Melin of Grace," said Zees aloud, "I am Zees."

Melin sought for the feeling of Goroin, and it was true.

"My friends know," Zees said. "Sit quietly. Don't be afraid."

"Where is Goroin?" Melin asked.

"He is here, safe. He will flow once again when the time comes, as you will flow." She allowed Goroin to communicate.

"It is true, Melin," he said. "We have lost. Should Don discover the method, don't struggle. That way lies madness." He knew if he had not been momentarily shocked by the numbing of his body the struggle for control would have been much more severe.

"Then we are lost," Melin of Grace said, and in her femaleness she wept.

Don Duckworth was weeping like a woman, his face contorted, tears large and wet.

"It is not Don who weeps," Zees explained.

"Zees," Breed said, "maybe you'd better start from the first."

She did. She saw doubt on Breed's face, at first, and then Ellen began to show more and more interest. She concentrated on Ellen. And when she had made the situation as clear as was possible, she made her suggestion.

"There's only one way you're going to understand and to believe," she said. "You'll have to experience it."

"No way," Breed said.

"I can tell you, show you, how to prevent losing control," Zees said. "Ellen, look at me and concentrate." She sent, she could sense the complicated structure of Ellen's brain. She made stimuli there. Ellen jerked.

"What the hell?" Ellen asked.

"You feel?"

"Yes."

"This is the area," Zees said, causing Ellen to be aware. "Hold, thus, and you cannot be controlled."

"My God," Ellen said. "It's as if I can see into my own brain."

"Ellen, will you try?" Zees asked.

"Zees, it's scary, some alien life force mucking around in your brain."

"I know, darling, I know," Zees said, "but that way

you'll know them, and you'll be giving your knowledge to one of them. They're going to need all the help they can get. And there's no danger.''

"Breed, I trust her," Ellen said. "I think it is Zees and not one of them.''

"Breed, keep your weapon ready, if you're still doubtful," Zees said.

"Yes," Breed said, doubtful indeed.

"The Longlegs are awake," Zees said. "Ellen, if you'll go unlock the bay, Mank the Soft will come with you. You'll need a medical kit.''

Mank and Ords, having revived, had been briefed by Zees. Mank was a bit puzzled, but she obeyed and followed Ellen to the bridge.

"I know not this way of flowing," Mank protested, when it was explained.

"It will work," both Goroin and Melin told her.

Ellen made a simple connection, needles in both Mank's arm and her own, a tube between, and when she pumped blood from Mank into her own arm Mank flowed and found herself and began to learn.

"It's true, Breed," Ellen said. "It's just as Zees said.''

The Longlegs from which Mank had flowed stood nervously, looking for somewhere to browse. Breed was impressed by the almost instant change, from intelligent, alert awareness to a sort of bovine indifference.

The flow was reversed and Mank the Soft was Longlegs.

A reluctant Breed had a visitor. He was startled at first, and then he came to admire the fierce independence of Ords the Freerunner. And then Ords was Longlegs again.

Melin allowed Don to communicate. "Any further messages from home?" was his first question. There had been none.

"I think we'll all agree that the situation is a bit different now," Zees said. "We don't know exactly what's going on back on Earth, but I think it's safe to say that whatever it is, a slight delay in our return won't have too much effect. I think we should stay here awhile longer. I think we should do all we can to help the Longlegs prepare for the cold. It may be futile in the long run, but it's going to take a couple of hundred years, at the earliest, for the cold to ice over every-thing. If we can give them a start, help them prepare to survive, then in the time it takes for full icing to happen surely we can find somewhere for them, surely we can con-vince the people at home that they're worth helping.''

"And if it's war at home?" Breed asked.

"Are you so eager to go home and fight?" Zees asked.

"I'm an officer in the Space Service," Breed said.

"As we all are," Zees said. "Would the four of us really make a difference?"

"I'll vote we stay for a few weeks," Ellen said.

"Don?" Zees asked.

"We can use the ship's facilities to make some real tools," Don said. "Stone axes don't make cabin building very easy."

14

It was Ellen who found a simple solution to the problem of flowing into a springer only to have to spend years growing the body and training it to perform. She found that the existence of a life force in a springer body stimulated certain glands. Goroin flowed into a few springer bodies, stimulated, flowed back to join Zees. Growth began immediately, and by the injection of chemical solutions growth was accelerated, the springer growing almost before one's eyes. Soon there would be a bank of fully developed springers ready for flow when one of the people aged.

In the meantime, the work continued. Gleaming metal axes and saws felled the ferntrees. Great Ones used their strength to move the logs. A settlement of log cabins formed quite rapidly, and, as the nights began to cool, the cabins were warmed by open fires in baked clay fireplaces.

The lifeboat went out day after day to search the planet for life. The free-roaming desert Longlegs sometimes took a little extra convincing, but there was no individual on the planet who could not feel and sense the change. Life was found in the form of food creatures, and the growing springers were filled and more pairs of hands were added to the work force.

When Goroin was satisfied that the search for life had been thorough enough, the population of the western area was just under five thousand. Goroin noted with interest that the long search did not turn up a single free-roaming Great One, making it almost certain that the Great One who had almost become Goroin the Great had been the last.

And it was the Great Ones who presented a real problem. It

had been decided to tell all that the world would soon be entering an ice age. The meetins were held in the ceremonial clearings which were maintained by the Great Ones, in spite of Goroin's urgings to abandon the old ceremonies. The Longlegs, having accepted Goroin's leadership, knowing the humans, believed. They could feel the chill in the nights. Some had flown in the lifeboat to see the ice building on the poles.

But being a Great One had, for all of the history of the people, been complete fulfillment.

"Are Goroin and the men from the far Earth jealous?" asked the outspoken Trinka the Lesser. "You ask us to abandon our Great Ones? How do we know it is not merely so that you, yourself, can be Great? How do we know that your friends from the far Earth can so surely predict the ice? I see no ice. I feel the warmth of the World."

"And you feel the chill in the night," Goroin said. "Then your blood thickens and you move slowly."

"Once when the clouds lifted and the sun came through I felt chill," Pudee the Helper said. "The chill passed."

"We'll just wait awhile, Goroin," Zees told him. "When they're so cold they can't move, then they'll believe."

The rains came. They came in a deluge which washed ash from the saturated clouds. They came in a dawn-world deluge which almost overwhelmed the settlement. But the cabins had been placed with foresight on a high plateau near the western woodlands. Each day work was required to remove a burden of slimy mud, and each day the rains came again and the oceans grew and great streams cut canyons through the once-arid desert. The volcanos in the south added more ash and more steam, and the heavens seemed to be made of water which cascaded down in pounding torrents. And then one day a weak sun shone through the cleansed clouds and the mud began to dry slowly and the chill crept into the blood of the Great Ones.

Breed took seeds from the stores on the *Maria* and planted them in the new, rich, volcanic topsoil. Wheat, oats, corn, melons, vegetables would become a part of the diet after the rains ceased and the sun was able to penetrate the clouds.

The summer was chill, but, in the western settlement, there

was no frost. Once again Don Duckworth began to think of going home. It pained him to have ignored an order, but seeing the progress of the Longlegs made it worthwhile. Now they fashioned warm garments from springer and food-creature skins. They made fired clay vessels in which to store water and food. In six months amazing progress had been made. Some Longlegs were working with soft metals, fashioning articles of gold. Under Breed's guidance the culture leaped past bronze and began to fashion crude tools of iron. A vein of coal was found near the surface and that fuel was added to wood to warm the cabins.

Breed was proud of his students. The Longlegs had abandoned their slothful ways and worked with a will. "Give me a few years," he said, "and I'll put them in space."

But much of the precipitation which had fallen had been in the form of snow and sleet in the northern and southern latitudes. The great icecaps were growing daily and the coming of winter brought crisis. It was to help Goroin meet it that Don had stayed, postponing the long-delayed trip home.

It was the first snow ever seen by the Great Ones, and, slowed by the cold, they bellowed in pain as it covered them, clung to their hides, slowing their blood, causing pain.

"It is time, my people," Goroin told them, joining them on their ceremonial grounds, bringing with him a store of fully grown springers. He had, at last, transferred back to a Longlegs, and rather enjoyed it. He especially enjoyed the nights, which were spent in his cabin with a sleek, well-fed, youthful, passionate Melin of Grace.

"It must be time," moaned a small Great One, lifting his chilled and aching feet one at a time to try to stamp warmth into them. "I will obey your wishes, Goroin."

One by one the Great Ones flowed. By long habit they had formed according to size. The younger ones flowed first, then they went up the line, until, at last, there were left only Pudee the Helper, largest of the Great Ones, and the proud Trinka the Lesser.

To make the job go faster the traditional eating ceremony had been abandoned and the flow was accomplished by blood flow, the tapping of veins being done by Ellen and Zees.

When it was Trinka's turn, she turned away.

"Come, Trinka," Zees said. She was in full communication with the people. In fact, she had taught the trick of mental communication to the other humans, and it was only the urgency of working with the Longlegs which prevented her from undertaking some interesting experiments. However, those experiments would be in a field which was totally unknown, and she didn't want to leap into anything without having had a chance for full study. The plight of the people was, for the moment, more in need of attention.

"I will be last," Trinka said.

"I am the greatest," Pudee said. "It is only right that I be the last."

Ellen, standing by one of Pudee's huge legs, skipped aside as the irritated Pudee shifted his weight. "Hey, big boy, watch it," she told him.

"This female has no right," Pudee said angrily. Once he had hoped to succeed Moulan as leader. Once he had been second-greatest and now he was greatest and his greatness was wasted because of change and Goroin and the men from the far Earth. And he was in pain. He ached with the cold and the snow clung to his hide and seemed to burn. And a mere female was defying him, trying to steal the very last of his glories.

"Why not do it together?" Zees suggested. It had been a long day and she was tired. She was in no mood to be kept in the cold by childishness in the form of two freezing dinosaurs.

"I must not flow," Trinka wailed. "I have fertile seed. I must not flow before my eggs come."

"Trinka, Trinka," Zees said. "The eggs would only freeze."

"Flow now," Pudee said. "I, Pudee the Helper, who was made second in command by Goroin the Great, order it."

"I obey no orders from an excrement eater," Trinka the Lesser said.

Once, to show his dominance, Moulan the Strong had demanded such an act of Pudee. Until now, none of the people had had the courage to remind him. He saw the red of anger and for a moment he was still a Great One and would not accept so enormous an insult. Behind the sudden swing of his tail was the inertial force of tons of flesh and the power of a half-dozen Earthside elephants. The blow caught the chilled and sluggish Trinka the Lesser by surprise, and she toppled, moaning in shock and pain. Under Zees' feet the snow was slippery, and as she yelled in surprise and tried to leap aside she slipped, scrambling as the clifflike bulk fell almost as if in slow motion and hoping she was going to be able to scramble free. Her gloved hands were digging and her feet pushing even as she felt a great blow which left her in blackness.

She was in a dark, cold place and she could not get out. The weight of a world was on her and there was pain which hazed her mind. She thought she could hear Ellen's voice.

"Lift, you excrement eater," Goroin was yelling at Pudee the Helper, who was trying to lift the stunned body of Trinka the Lesser. "Don't worry about hurting Trinka, bite and lift."

Don, who had been observing, was holding Zees' hand. He could see that she was badly hurt. The inside fluid collectors of the suit, worn for warmth, were busy collecting blood. Ellen looked up at him, and she was weeping. The suit was crushed terribly. When Pudee managed to lift Trinka's bulk a little, she and Don pulled the crushed body free and Ellen tore open the suit.

"Oh, no, oh, no," Ellen was sobbing.

He could see that it was hopeless. The weight of the dinosaur had smashed down on her from the breast down. The ribcage was smashed and flattened. The stomach was ruptured by sheer weight, showing dark and pulsing things inside. He could not bear to look.

He stood, looked at the dazed Pudee, and felt like unleashing his weapon on full burn. Trinka the Lesser was trying to get to her feet. One of her legs was obviously broken. But he didn't care because that crushed thing in the snow was Zees. Zees, a woman who had been with him almost every minute for three years, a woman unlike any woman he'd ever known, and not all the skill which Ellen had would alter the fact that, although her heart was still beating, she was dead.

Goroin knelt beside her. "Zees, my friend," he said,

making his sendings as powerful as he could. Her closed eyes did not move.

"Ellen, can you make her conscious?" he asked.

"It's no use. She'd only feel pain," Ellen said.

"She must be conscious. It is the only chance," Goroin said.

"Leave her alone, damn you," Don said, jerking Goroin to his feet and shoving him away.

"You don't understand," Goroin said. "We have talked, Zees and I. She can do it."

"Do you mean she can flow?" Ellen asked, not daring to hope.

"Yes," Goroin said. "Melin, quickly, bring me the female."

The half-grown springer which had been for Trinka the Lesser was led forward.

"I told you to leave her alone," Don said, knowing only his own agony as he watched Zees' chest flutter as her heart prepared to die.

"Don," Ellen said calmly. "We can try."

"Human beings don't flow," Don said angrily. "I will not let you cause her more pain. Let her die without knowing."

"My friend, I beg you," Goroin said.

"No. I told you no, damn you," Don said. He dropped to his knees, took her in his arms, saw her blood oozing out, saw the whiteness of exposed bones. Her heart was going into its last sharp spasms. Goroin knew that within minutes that splendid brain would be deprived of oxygen and would begin to die. He leaned quickly and seized Ellen's weapon, thumbed it to low stun, let the beam take Duckworth full in the face.

"Goroin," Ellen screamed.

"Make her conscious," he ordered, the weapon on Ellen.

"Yes, yes," she said. "We must try." She took the stimulant from her medical kit and mainlined it into the heart, along with a huge dose of painkiller. Zees' eyes fluttered. She screamed in agony, and then her eyes were wide.

"My friend Zees," Goroin said.

Her lips tried to move. He searched and found her, alive, frightened. "As we have talked, my friend. As I have told you."

"Yes," she said to him. "Quickly."

The connection was made. Ellen pumped and blood flowed from Zees' arm into the placidly waiting Longlegs.

"Now, my friend," Goroin said, showing her the way, guiding, coaxing, urging.

She rode the world's largest roller coaster and fell forever and was lost and there was Goroin's voice, coaxing, guiding, and she climbed slowly, slowly, weak and only half aware, and the dying heart had stopped. Quickly the cells of the brain began to die, and she was still lost and there was the soft voice urging, showing, and then there was light.

"I am," Zees said.

She looked down on the crushed and bloody thing which had been Zees, and her double-lidded eyes filled.

"What have you done?" Don asked, coming out of stun, moving feebly.

"Don, Don," she said, going to him. He started to pull away from the female Longlegs, and then his eyes went wide.

"Zees?" he asked.

"Don, it's much, much better than that," she said, as the body of Zees jerked and was still. She knelt beside him in the snow, feeling the youthful vigor of her new body, knowing that it had a vitality which she had not felt in years. "Heck," she said, her long snout showing a toothy grin, "I'm probably the first Earthwoman in a century to have a fur coat."

But she was not feeling quite as flippant about it as she sounded. She was just beginning to realize the significance of the swift events of the past few minutes. She was Zees, of Earth, and she'd been a long way from home but she'd never doubted that she would return. Now she was Zees, woman of Earth and Longlegs, and what would happen if she went home? They'd want to study and probe and poke and in the end they would put her in the equivalent of a zoo and—

"Welcome, my friend," Goroin said.

She looked at him. He was only slightly larger than she and his body was not yet fully mature. She looked like that, she was thinking, furred, a sort of kangarooish thing with a long snout and big, tearing teeth and large eyes—which were not all bad, she found, looking around to see better than she'd seen with human eyes.

"It's quite a nice body," Goroin said.

"Don't get fresh with me, young man," she said.

"My God, Zees," Don said, standing.

"There's work to be done, kiddies," she said. "Ellen, transfer these two hardheads before they melt."

Pudee the Helper and Trinka, who was in pain from her broken leg, offered no further resistance.

15

"DON, there's nothing else you can do here," Zees said.

A weak sun flooded the plateau with a light which, in contrast to the former gloom of the planet, was cheerful. But there was a deadliness in that light, too, for the greenhouse effect which had kept the planet warm was gone with the clouds which had rained mud and water. The cold of deep space was creeping in. The weather pattern was much like that of Earth now, with the weak sun drawing moisture from the newly formed lakes and streams and the oceans and letting it fall again as snow and sleet and frozen rain. The glaciation of the north and south was well under way, and each night that passed saw more of the heat pass away into space.

"I know," Don said. "We've done all we can."

He knew that he had to go. Breed and Ellen were ready. The ship was ready.

"You can still change your mind," he said.

"No, Don. I won't go back like this. I won't go as a freak." She had given it long and serious thought. And she'd wept with the reality of being totally cut off from all that she'd ever known. "You know it makes more sense for me to stay. I can help. And it's not all bad, you know. I've come to love the people. They're gentle and intelligent. There's a feeling of unity here which I've never experienced before on so large a scale. You know how it was with the four of us alone on the *Maria*? Well, it's like that with all of us here."

"Yeah, well," he said.

"Just go, Don. Go and get things straightened out. You all have something to contribute now."

"Well, we'd make good spies," he chuckled, thinking of the ability which Zees had taught them. "We'll be the only telepaths on Earth."

"It's a tool which can be used for understanding," Zees said. "When men can look into each other's minds, to see the truth, that will mean an end to greed and selfishness."

"Well, maybe you're just a little bit too optimistic," he said. "But we'll try, Zees. And I promise you that I'll be back. I'll get back out here at the first opportunity and I'll bring a ship so big we can shift the entire population. You should be able to hold out for a few years."

They did not lack for food. The flesh of all the Great Ones had been frozen. It had been taken to the north by the lifeboat and, in preparation for the departure of the *Maria*, shifted back south as the cold advanced and made a permanent deep-freeze of the western settlement. The flesh of the Great Ones, alone, was enough food to last for a long time.

"I still think we should leave you the lifeboat," Don said.

"No, now, we've discussed that. I don't know enough to keep it in repair. It's not big enough to shift all of us. So when it's time to move to the south we'll all move together."

"That's where I'll look for you when I come back," he said.

"I'll be waiting."

He looked at her and grinned. "You know, you're sort of sexy in a way, with that cute long snout and the big watery eyes."

She laughed, and it was a dead giveaway. She was fighting tears. They rolled from her large eyes.

The party was held in the house which had been built for Zees. Ellen brought down booze, and it was discovered that Longlegs were cheap drunks, never having been exposed to alcohol. Goroin tried to drown his sadness at losing his friends and became comically drunk, and once he wailed like a baby when he found that he could not stand up, then he laughed, for sitting wasn't all that bad. Zees, feeling the effects on her Longlegs body, limited her intake.

One by one the people came to bid farewell to the three

who would go. Many times the promise to return, to rescue all from the cold, was repeated. And then it was morning and the lifeboat lifted and in the snow Zees stood, her body covered in her own fur and the fur of animals.

"Don't weep," Melin said, putting an arm around Zees.

"Perhaps just a little," Zees said.

She wanted to be alone, so she went to her cabin. A bed had been fashioned from furs and leaves. She lay on it and could sense it when the blink generators jumped, felt the twinge as if she'd been aboard, and then she was more alone than she'd ever been in her life. She wept more than a little, and then she rose, straightened her shoulders, and went in search of Goroin.

The earthquakes which had once plagued the planet were almost nonexistent now. When they came they were mere tremors. Overflights in the lifeboat had shown a great lessening in volcanism, and the volcanoes which were still active were venting mostly steam, to be raised aloft, chilled, and turned into more snow and sleet. The great glaciers were edging southward. Slowly the glutted oceans were being reduced by evaporation, the megatons of water being added to the ice caps. The permanent snow line extended far to the south now.

The people would stay in the original settlement for a time, until most of the flesh of the Great Ones had been consumed. Then the first of the long treks would begin. The days passed slowly, but there was always work. The springers, who would soon become the only source of food, were surprisingly hardy little creatures. They loved the snow, and at any time during the daylight hours one could see them in their hundreds leaping and playing. They fed on dried forage stored in the barns. The food for the springers was more important than the flesh of the Great Ones, and when it was almost gone it would be time to move to the south, where some forests still existed.

Goroin was the leader. Zees made no attempt to usurp his authority, but he looked to her for advice. She spent a lot of time with him and Melin in either her house or theirs, and when Melin gave birth to four healthy springers to be added to the pool she was on hand, although birth was so effortless that Melin needed no help.

"When will you choose?" Melin asked her, when the new brood was feeding from Melin's swollen teats.

"There is time," Zees said.

"Many have eyes for you," Goroin said.

"Soon." She was not quite ready for that. She lived inside a healthy body which had healthy urges, but she was not quite ready. There was time. Then she would do her duty and contribute to the springer pool. As yet, she was still human enough to cringe to think that she would become fertile and give birth, and that her offspring, at least most of them, would be eaten. It was the way of the World, but she could not, just yet, accept it.

The cold was with them always. It had been only a month since the Earthship left, and the average temperature had dropped significantly. The fodder stores for the springers was slowly being depleted. It was time.

It was a silent people who left their first settlement, dragging food supplies on sleds, bundled into their furs. The springers leaped and cavorted about the long series of caravans and the sun shone weakly over the snowfields and the direction was always to the south. They reached the slope of the tumbled scarp within days, traveling fast. The slope was covered with snow, but made for difficult going. And then there were the high mountains and a deeper cold and thin air and at last a view from the pass selected from the memories of Roag the Rememberer. The mountains had been altered, but the pass was still there, and ahead there was only more snow, which began to thin, to cover the ground with a less dense blanket. There was, by contrast, a hint of warmth. And then there was the blasted forest with vegetation still surviving.

Once again axes rang and saws bit into the trees and houses went up with the skill of practice. The springers were waxing fat when Don Duckworth returned.

He came without warning. Zees was at work, pulling one end of a crosscut saw, and she had just stepped back to see a ferntree fall when she felt it and looked up and saw the familiar shape of the *Santa Maria*'s lifeboat. Others saw it quickly, and a vocal shout of greeting went up as the lifeboat lowered and settled into the village clearing. Zees had been running as fast as she could, fearing the worst, thinking that something had happened to the ship and now the others would be stranded with her.

But her heart leaped with excitement when she recognized, even in the suit, the movements of Don Duckworth. She almost bowled him over. She danced him around, making meaningless sounds, and then she halted, looked through the visor into his eyes. He had changed. He had aged terribly.

"Don't worry," he said. "It's just that I've been a few weeks without the nutrient." Deprived of the medication which stopped his biological clock, age had come on him suddenly. He almost looked his seventy-plus years.

"Don?" she asked.

"Not now," he said. "I want to see Goroin and Melin and all the others, then I'll tell all."

Most of the people had gathered around the boat. Goroin pushed his way through, clasped Don in his arms. Melin bowed. The people hailed him, bowed, showed their pleasure and their hope. He had returned long before anyone had even dared think he would. Problems were no more. Don had returned and they would be moved to a place of warmth and plenty.

He could see the hope, could feel it, and he was saddened. He knew that he could not allow it to grow, to make disappointment more severe.

"My friends," he said, "I come with sad words."

Zees tried to look into his mind. But he had been working, and his was a human brain, and she could not penetrate. He sent her a private message. "Yes, I have blocked you out, Zees."

"Speak, my friend," Goroin said. "Your sad words will not lessen our joy at seeing you once more."

"In a moment, my friend," he said. He turned. He closed his mind to all but Zees, and she could not help but admire his control, while dreading what he was going to say.

"They're dead," he told her.

"Breed? Ellen?" The pain of it came to her.

"All," he said. "Everyone."

"Oh, God," she said.

"It had begun when we came to the last jump," he said. "Both sides were promising not to use nukes. Breed felt that he had to go down. Ellen, too. She said she could be of use, being a doctor, because the fighting was heavy in Europe and the Middle East. Our side was having the best of it. I begged them not to go, because I knew that they wouldn't take defeat, that they'd send the missiles up. But they went."

"And some fool did it," Zees said.

"I told them I'd promised to come back," Don said. "I took the boat. I saw the first salvo go up just as the *Maria* was lowering down at Idaho Port. Then they all went up and—" He could not speak.

"I'll tell them," Zees said. She spoke to them, all of them. "My people. There will be no help from the Far Earth, because the war that we feared has come, and the Earth has been made more deadly than our own planet. So now we are alone."

She did not give them all of her thoughts, for she was thinking: We are the last intelligence. We live while billions have died. And we, too, will die when the glaciers meet at the equator.

"So be it," Goroin said. "We are alone, but we are alive."

Don Duckworth, human, was no more. He had resisted flowing as long as he could, but his aging body, deprived of the magic of medication, was doing its best to catch up with his actual age. He grew tired of feeling the cold so severely, of being a feeble old man and not being able to do his share. With the aid of Goroin, he flowed into the body of a nearly grown springer and tried out his new legs in a little dance which caused the people to laugh.

And it was then that Zees chose. It was then that her bed was no longer cold and empty and, after weeping together for the fate of the billions of Earth, they loved, for they were alive and there was still hope.

The volcanic activity of the southern sea sent some heat into the air. The sea, with volcanic activity pouring molten lava into it, remained warm for many years, and then the volcanic activity was slowing and in the winters the sea came to be covered by ice to a great distance from shore. The people, now as far south as it was possible to go, without crossing the warm zone and going into the cold of the lower hemisphere, found a new source of food in the sea. Springers fed on seaweed. Life was good, even as the ice advanced and each summer was shorter.

When the ice, in winter, reached all the way across the southern ocean, Zees was in her third Longlegs body. The years had been good. They had known that it was inevitable, so when, one summer, the ice did not thaw and then thickened so that cutting through to reap the decreasing seaweed crop became more and more difficult, they were forced to turn to their last resource. They made the springer bank last for five more years.

And there was then nothing from pole to pole but the ice and it glistened in weak sunlight which would not become strong enough to melt the ice, to put moisture back into the desiccated air, until a star passed through a cycle which, by best estimate, could be no less than a million years.

"A work unit is on the surface now," Arlos said. "I have instructed them to remove the overburden from a section of the settlement. I was sure you'd be interested."

"Yes, of course," Lee said, but he was thinking of the ship and the written material.

A small boat was readied. Lee felt awkward in the heavy suit, but soon became accustomed to it. It was designed to use automatic power to make movements feel natural.

Lani chattered happily as the boat fell away from the bulk of the X&A ship and arced downward. The atmosphere was almost cloudless. The new sun, once the sixth planet, was on the opposite side of the primary. Already, however, the additional energy of the second sun was generating melting at the equator, Lani showed him on the boat's instruments. They were flying low now and the water-vapor content in the air was increasing as they neared the equator and the site of the discovery.

"Does an X&A ship always carry such machinery?" Lee asked, as Lani flew the boat low and slow over the site.

"Oh, no," she said. "We had it blinked in from Trojan V. The large thing is a heater. It melted the ice, and the other things are pumps to remove the water."

The result was a hole, sides perpendicular, extending into the ice for some two hundred feet. At the bottom he saw the gleam of metal, a crude log cabin. The sight was so unexpected, so contradictory, that he felt a little weak with anticipation.

Lani lowered the small boat with a casual ease, halted its plunge inches above the icy floor of the pit, then let it settle. A young man greeted them as they stepped out of the boat.

"This is Laru the Healer," Lani said. "He entered the ship."

"I touched nothing, sir," Laru said. "I would ask your permission to be allowed to accompany you, however."

"I think you've earned that right," Holland Lee said. "And you, Lani."

"We had to do some force lubrication before we could get the hatch open," Laru the Healer explained, as he led the way toward the ship, not much larger than the small runabout aboard which Lee had made the descent to the surface. "It's in surprisingly good condition, considering that it's been under the ice for thousands of years.''

"Have you people done any dating of the ice at all?'' Lee asked.

"Not yet, sir,'' Laru said. "We have a crew working on that now. We should have some preliminary figures for you soon.''

"Thank you,'' Lee said. "The hatch operates now?''

They were standing beside the ship. Laru reached out. He was not suited, having the advantage of his own body armor. The cold did not penetrate, and the thin, dry air was, to him, quite heady. In a pinch he could have existed for days on a tenth as much.

Holland Lee held his breath and stuck his head inside. He was disappointed. He saw the usual mass of dials and gauges and switches and buttons and acceleration chairs.

"It could be one of our own,'' he said. "Something from a space museum.''

"I noted that, sir,'' Laru said.

He entered. He looked more closely at the control panel and felt his face flush with excitement. "I don't suppose either of you attended Xanthos,'' he said.

"I was not so fortunate,'' Laru said.

"Nor was I,'' Lani added.

"No courses in the study of language?'' Lee asked, letting his eyes browse over the interior of the vessel.

They both indicated no. He saw the book, then. It was in a cubbyhole under the control panel.

"This, I take it,'' he said, indicating the book, "is the written matter?''

"Yes, sir,'' Lani said.

He touched it. It seemed to be in quite good condition. He removed it ever so carefully. He smiled. He felt a surge of pure elation. He had guessed right. Log cabins and a spaceship.

"Shall I read you the title of this book?'' he asked, looking through his visor at Lani.

"Do you mean you can? So soon?'' she asked.

"Of course. It's only old English. The title of this book is *Operating Manual for Class 27-C Lifeboat.*''

"Then it is one of ours?" Lani asked, her face showing disappointment.

"Yes, and no," Holland Lee said. "Lanu, you can tell your crew that this planet began to ice just over fifty-thousand New Years ago."

"Old Ones," Laru breathed. "It's an Old One ship."

"From the Earth," Holland Lee said, holding the operating manual in his hands as if it were a holy object. "From before the cataclysm. Perhaps they escaped at the last minute and settled here, only to be overcome by an ice age."

"If this ship could only speak," Laru said, awed. The destruction of the Earth had been so complete, the time span before reunion so long, that little remained of the old Earth culture save scattered inscriptions and some interesting ruins under the silt of a seabed.

"It can tell us much," Holland said. He sat in the command chair. "It tells us, by the configuration of this chair, that the Old Ones were of a size with me. It tells us that it was from North America, that area which was Rack's country. The controls tell us that they had fingers and thumbs just like ours—mine, that is."

He rose and began to look around. "They were far advanced in electronics, as witness the fact that this ship draws power from a blink drive, unrefined, of course, but using the same principle which drives our ships. This vessel was designed to carry four people comfortably." He had opened the hatch to the rear compartment. "And someone had a sense of neatness."

The sleep couches were folded neatly away. He opened one, felt the sheets, the covering. He chuckled, and held up a long brown hair. "At least one of those who traveled on this ship was a woman."

"Or a long-haired man," Lani said.

"Killjoy." Lee laughed. "I was enjoying being a time detective."

Everything was surprisingly well preserved. The cold had penetrated. The sheets of the couches were stiff, but not frozen, because there was no moisture in them. "We'll have to keep it refrigerated," he said.

"No problem," Lani said. "The cold bay of the *Gore* will hold it."

"It can all be dated," he said. "The materials of the bedthings, the metals. We'll have to move it to Xanthos, where we have the proper facilities."

"Would you like to take a look at the log cabin now, sir?" Lanu the Healer asked.

"No, no, not just yet. You two can run along, if you like. I'd like to take a closer look, and although you have the best of intentions you might accidentally spoil something in here."

He was alone. He stood in the living quarters and mused. "I wish you could speak," he said to the long-dead ship. "I do wish you could."

He spent some time reading labels. He tried the old words on his tongue. Some were simple words: liquid waste, fire extinguisher, water. Others were more technical: generator flux, core amperes, chamber amplitude. It was old English. The labels gave the ship the look of a military craft, designed to be operated by different crews, perhaps, everything labeled. It would make the engineering analysis of the ship easy.

He began to poke into closed areas, hatches, vents, and was amused to find the sanitary facilities to be crude, but much like those aboard a small modern ship. There'd be some work to be done. Captain Arlos might feel that it was inevitable for different cultures, should different cultures exist, to arrive at the blink principle if they worked with electronics and space vehicles, but he did not agree. When the first men went out from Earth in primitive ships they must have carried with them this same technology, for much of UP advances could be traced back, he felt, to equipment aboard this one small boat.

Once again the old questions would be raised. How could a culture forget its origin? How could the location of the home planet, old Earth, be forgotten? If men had ships like these, with blink drives, why had not someone gone back? The theory was that the small expedition had landed on Terra II in desperate condition, that there was a return to primitivism, that technology had been forgotten and that there'd been a long, long crawl back into space. And yet this crude and ancient vessel pointed the way toward the sophistication of a ship like the *Bradley J. Gore*, which could reduce huge spaces of the galaxy to a blink jump which took a fraction of a second.

Small as it was, the ancient ship was a treasure trove. In a closet he found garments. He judged them to be uniforms, for they were of a kind, white, one-piece, but of two basic sizes, and the top portion of the smaller garments were cut fuller to accommodate the female breasts. On a hunch, he looked for pockets, felt inside them when he found them, feeling almost guilty as if he were invading the bedchamber of strangers and prowling. He was rewarded in his search by finding a small notebook in one of the larger uniforms. A name was stamped on the cover in gold.

Capt. Donald R. Duckworth, U.S.S.S.

The notebook was fragile, and he looked only at the first page. It was, apparently, a record of blink coordinates. A space engineer could, possibly, trace the voyage of the vessel from those figures. He replaced it where he had found it and continued his search.

He found the treasure in a small cubbyhole under one of the couches.

3

THE sun, Xanthos, was a kind one. The stable world knew no seasons in the temperate zones. The temperature was always at or near seventy-five degrees, and classrooms were designed to blend and be a part of the parklike campus. Around the campus the world of the computers rose to multistoried heights.

Professor Holland Lee's Advanced Seminar in Alien Languages had met three times in the new semester. It was, Lee thought, an outstanding group of young people.

When Lee entered, the class stood in politeness, then took seats as he sat down behind his desk and looked out over the variety of human faces.

"So," he said, "how did we fare with Old English Longhand?"

"Professor, it *is* an alien language," said the girl who had become, in spite of his reluctance to show favoritism, his pet. Her name was Helena. She was of Selbelle III, his home planet.

"But you did get the hang of it, I trust," he said.

"At three o'clock this morning I could begin to read it," Helena said.

"Perhaps, then, you would like to begin the discussion," Lee said.

Helena rose. She smiled. "I'm sure that you and the computers will be pleased to know that I agree with the analysis, that the document is the personal log, or diary, of a woman of old Earth."

"We are pleased," Lee smiled back.

142

"She was a lovely, warm person," Helena said. "She faced a tragedy which was so complete that I can't even imagine it. She lost herself—"

"Only her body," said a dark young Tigian.

"—and her world," Helena said. "She died knowing that humanity had been destroyed, or, at least, thinking that it had been destroyed. She had no way of knowing that some survived the atomic war on Earth to become the mutated forms."

"Yes," Lee said. The Tigian, Barnard, was holding up his hand. "Barnard?"

"She also had no way of knowing that some of the Old Ones had survived in space," he said.

"We are proof of that," Lee said.

"Aside from being a personal document of great poignancy," Barnard said, "the diary of the woman called Zees is an important historical find."

"How so?" Lee asked. "Darcie?"

Darcie, of Zede II, rose. She was a tall blond girl. "We know something of the root of the cataclysm," she said. "Overpopulation. A struggle for the meager and already depleted resources of the old Earth. We have mention in the diary of a fleet of exploration which went out from Earth before the blink drive was fully developed, and how it was thought to be lost. I am sure in my mind that the exploration fleet was the source of the development of human civilization on Terra II."

"Sir," said Lirus, from the outplanet New Texas, "I think the most important information in the work is that life has formed independently on a planet other than Earth."

"A good point," Lee said. "You are assuming with that statement that my wife and her people are products of the old Earth, are you not?"

"Yes," Lirus said.

"And he's forgetting the Dead Worlders," said Lani, who had decided to take advantage of her status as a faculty wife to seek an advanced degree. "Just in case," she had told Holland with a smile, "you grow tired of me and I have to go back to work."

"And yet it is an important point," Lee said. "And a

tragedy that the Longlegs, as Zees and her people called them, had to become extinct."

"May I?" asked Parisha, Power Giver.

"Speak," Lee said.

"I am most intrigued by the not too well detailed hints of the mental powers developed by the Old Ones of Earth after having been occupied by the life force of the Longlegs."

"Mental language, telepathy, is not a strange concept to you," Lee said.

"True," Parisha said. "But we people of old Earth have been a part of the UP for over two hundred years. To this date we have not been able to teach, or develop, telepathic ability among you Old Ones."

"True," Lee said.

"I have planned to ask your permission to do my term paper on this aspect of the journal," Parisha said. "I see a sort of parallel between the hints which Zees gave regarding the methods she used to overcome Goroin and the scant hints about the working of the Bertt drive in the Cygnus Papers. From mere mentions and hints scientists developed the power invented by Bertt. Perhaps, from scant hints in the Worthless Papers, I can—" She paused. "But I assume too much."

"Not at all," Lee said. "You have my permission. If you need extra computer time, please call on me."

"Thank you, sir," Parisha said. "If we can locate the area of the brain which Zees hinted at, break the barrier, then, perhaps, all will be able to communicate without words."

"And put me out of business." Lee laughed.

"I have a question for the class," said Lani, after getting the nod from Holland. "It's a multifaceted question. One, were the Longlegs immortal? Two, why were the individual life units, which they called life force, so limited on Worthless? Three, when there was no more food and the Longlegs died, and the life units melted, what happened to them? Are they still floating, or whatever, over the ice of the planet? Are they aware at all? Or have they truly died?"

"I, too, have considered that question," said Parisha the Power Giver. "In fact, Lani, I wanted to ask you and Professor Lee, having been on the planet, if you ever felt anything, a presence, a hint of something."

"Not I," Lee said. "Lani?"

"Nor I," she said. "I'll admit that after Dr. Lee read the journal and I knew the story I found myself looking over my shoulder at times, but, no, I never felt a presence, or a hint of a presence."

"We can't be sure," Lee said, "but it's been over fifty thousand years."

"But the life force was strong. When Roag the Rememberer melted, some of him remained, enough so that Goroin could share his memories. I think that the life unit was the same, that Roag was Goroin. What would happen if when we begin to settle Worthless, and animals are taken there, we wake up some morning to find a cow speaking to us through telepathy?"

"For that reason, we men being so xenophobic, the planet has been put off limits to visitors other than the official caretaker crew," Lee said.

"It was a dead planet," Lani said. "You could feel it. There was nothing, nothing. The life force was not strong enough to survive. We have hints of that in the melt of Roag the Rememberer. He lost most of himself in a short time. Fifty thousand years? I don't think we can expect to ever speak to a Longlegs in the form of a cow."

A bell rang. Lee rose. "We will continue this discussion tomorrow."

Darcie of Zede II looked at Parisha the Power Giver. "I don't think I'd like to settle Worthless," she said. "The mere thought of being taken over by a being which eats its own young. Ugg."

Lani met Holland outside the classroom, and they walked toward the cafeteria together. "How do you like being a schoolgirl again?" he asked.

"Hmmm," she said. "My Advanced Physics teacher is very handsome."

"Wench," he said, reaching down to put his hand on her head. A lot of eyebrows had been raised when he married a Thumber.

"But not as handsome as you," she said.

"Ah," he said, "I knew you were intelligent. That's why I married you."

BOOK THREE

The Fishers of Men

IN stygian blackness the fish moved lazily, nearing a volcanic vent on the floor of the sea. It settled, hard, thick scales making clicks on the tip of exposed and hardened lava. It glowed, forming its own light, and the seabed near the vent came to life in color, stalky tubeworms waved, showed their scarlet bodies outside the protective tube. The fish browsed on leafy things and then moved closer to the vent, where water heated by the liquid magma of the interior exited into the chill, creating an oasis of life.

The fish selected, and nosed down. A large shellfish opened itself. The fish snout probed and sharp teeth ate. The fish moved, and another shellfish opened its protective shell to be devoured, and then the treat was over. Even in the heat of the vent water it took a long time to grow the shellfish.

The fish ceased to glow, all light disappeared, and the blackness was absolute. But there was movement in the blackness, other fish, moving lazily. They gathered. One glowed briefly, and then there was only the dark.

"They are back."

"Yes."

Above them the chill of a mile of black water and then the ice, a mile thick.

The fish were of a-size. Long ago it had been decided to abandon the larger forms. Food was scarce under the ice and the eons stretched before them.

"When?"

Now and then a fish would glow. The gathering grew until the area around the vent of Zees was filled with them.

"We had expected to wait," Zees said.

"They say it has been fifty thousand of their years," said Goroin. "We have waited."

"And now the ice melts," Don said. "We can't measure it"—he could not even measure time in that eternal blackness—"but it melts. They say it does. They measure. Streams run from the glaciers. The thickness of the ice over the sea is being assaulted by warmer water. We have waited. We can wait a bit longer rather than take risks."

"He is right, Goroin," Zees said. "We faced a million years of blackness. Now we can look forward to the light in just decades of their years."

"They are men, as you were once men of the Earth," said Moulan. "Can we dominate?"

"Moulan, Once Strong," said Melin, "you doubt? You doubt when the force has survived? When we have spent so long in the darkness perfecting the force? When it is no longer necessary to be eaten? Now we choose, we flow. Now we control from a distance." She demonstrated by controlling a tubeworm, causing it to extend its tender body to be nibbled.

"We can control," Zees said.

Goroin laughed. "Once you would have said that would not be right," he said.

In the beginning, some had gone mad, and it was the work of years, uncounted and unregistered years, to bring them back to sanity.

"What is right?" Zees asked. "The World cares not for right. The universe cares not for right. We live, and that is right, and we have existed in blackness and cold and soon the ice will melt and they will come in numbers."

"We will have to plan a way to be close," Trinka said. "In order to flow."

"Fear not," Zees said. "They are men. Men are creatures of water worlds. Where there is water there are fish. Mark my words, my people. When the ice melts and the water is exposed man will be there and he will have in his hand some mechanical device, some means of taking food from the sea. Man is an eater, and he is fond of fish."

"We will give the fisherman a thrill," Don chuckled, "by showing him our strength, by fighting."

"And then," said Zees. "Ah, and then."

ZACH HUGHES is the pen name of Hugh Zachary, who, with his wife Elizabeth, runs a book factory in North Carolina. Hugh quit a timeclock job in 1963 and turned to writing full-time. He is the author of a number of well-received science fiction novels, and together with Elizabeth, he has turned out many fine historical romances, as well as books in half a dozen other fields.

Hugh Zachary has worked in radio and tv broadcasting and as a newspaper feature writer. He has also been a carpenter, run a charter fishing boat, done commercial fishing, and served as a mate on an anchor-handling tugboat in the North Sea oil fields.

Hugh's science fiction novels, KILLBIRD and PRESSURE MAN, are available in Signet editions.

BOOK TWO

The Sunmakers

_____

1

THE Paulus Chair of Alien Study at Xanthos University was a plum coveted by scholars of a hundred planets. For a century, after the chair was endowed by the teacher of literature who had been instrumental in translating the Cygnus Papers, the first alien manuscript known to man, the position had been claimed by scholars from either Terra II or Xanthos. There was considerable consternation in scholastic and governmental circles when young Holland Lee took the honored chair of the great teachers. Lee did not have, according to his critics, the scientific background required by the position. He was from Selbelle III, a planet noted for poets and artists, not for serious scholars.

There were many who felt that Holland Lee would show his lack of background when the first crisis blew up, and there was, in fact, some doubt in the minds of certain members of Headquarters Staff of Exploration and Alien Search about Lee's being the proper man to send out in the field when the X&A ship, UPX *Bradley J. Gore*, while making a routine survey of a potentially habitable planet, discovered an ancient spaceship under two hundred feet of ice.

Actually, it was what was inside the ancient and tiny ship which caused High Admiral Brunner Johns to send the blink-stat which put Holland Lee aboard a sleek and deadly cruiser which had never fired its impressive weapons except in practice and delivered him to X&A Headquarters to see the accumulation of paperwork before blinking outward into a previously very uninteresting portion of the galaxy.

Admiral Johns limited the first meeting to himself, Holland
Lee and two aides. As in all matters regarding possible
contact with an alien society there was a label of Urgent-
Urgent Secret-Secret on all material relating to the find.

Admiral Johns was an impressive man. A Tigian, well over
six feet, dark from the hot Tigian sun, full-bearded in an age
where beards were rare, he was, Holland Lee thought, just
the sort of man Lee would like to have in command if there
were really scary aliens out there somewhere, or if the
nonhumanoids who had, so many mysterious centuries ago,
blasted the Dead Worlds came swarming back into the United
Planets galaxy from the mystery into which they had disappeared.

Lee, himself, was almost dapper. He dressed with a dignity
commensurate with his important chair at the most prestigious
university in all the UP, but he had been blessed or cursed
with a face which looked younger than its years. He had a
slightly upturned nose, a full mouth, and dark-brown eyes
which tended to squint behind his old-fashioned framed glasses.

Admiral Johns, upon first seeing Lee, began to feel that
perhaps his staff had been right in classing Lee as a light-
weight. It wouldn't be the first time that some man had
politicked himself into a position he was not qualified to
hold. But the Chair of Alien Study at Xanthos was the logical
place to go. The man who held that chair had access to the
Xanthos computers which had cracked the alien language of
the Cygnus manuscript. The accepted translation of the altered warning inscription on the Dead Worlds was the work
of a man who had held the Paulus Chair, and the language
computers accessible to that chair had done the work on the
few written inscriptions found on Tom Thumb.

So, like the looks of the man or not, Admiral Johns had no
choice. He handled the introductions, escorted Lee to his
seat, then dumped it on him, handing him the sheaf of
papers.

"Take your time, professor," he said. "That ship's been
there a long time. It's not going anywhere."

Lee had only to read the first report from the *Bradley
Gore*.

Ref: Z-198-355-2034-C-212   X&A Restriction Code 1
                                 Blink Priority
                                 Urgent-Urgent

ORIGIN: UPX *Bradley J. Gore*, Sector C-789, Capt.
                 Arlos, F.S., Cmmd.

DES: Headquarters Exploration and Alien Search,
                 Attention: High Admiral Brunner Johns.

SUB: Archaeological find, III Planet, Lifezone
                 Potential, Class II-c Xanthos sun, possibly
                 previously inhabited humanoid.

REPORT: New Year 30,557, Month 2, Day 30 UPX.
                 Bradley J. Gore, engaged in routine survey
                 planets Class II-c Xanthos star, position
                 R-11-45, V-88-99, H-6-119, L-22-231; Sector
                 B-777, Tri-Chart Ref. B-923-442. (Survey
                 charts attached.)

PLANETARY   Planet permanently iced. .55 Oxygen
CONDITIONS: atmosphere. Water planet, iced.

LIFETYPE: Extinct. Definitely humanoid.

EXPLANATION   Survey readings indicated small mass
OF ABOVE: fabricated metal. Exploration revealed small
                 and very old vehicle with deep-space capability.
                 Further exploration revealed fabricated
                 dwellings made of logs from extinct trees.

REQUEST: Immediate dispatch experts to assess
                 archaeological finds, with special emphasis
                 written material aboard spaceship.

Holland Lee read no further. He felt his heart pause for a
moment. He could not stop himself from leaping to his feet.
It was, for Lee, a dream come true. He had read every word
ever written by or about Paulus, who had translated the
Cygnus Papers. In a vast confederation of planets where only
two languages were known, if one discounted the local
variations on the universal tongue, it was, he felt, even more
than he should have dared hope for. Of all men who had lived
in recorded history, only one, Paulus himself, had had the
opportunity to study a totally different and alien language.
And now this.

"Admiral," Lee said, trying to keep the excitement
contained, "I suggest that you order the cruiser to blink out

there with me as quickly as possible. That material could be very fragile."

"Relax, professor," Johns said. "The vessel has been resealed. The material is quite safe. It's been in cold storage for quite a few thousand years."

"Am I correct in assuming, since the planet involved is an ice planet, that the air is quite dry?" Lee asked.

"Yes," said one of the admiral's aides. "If you'll take time to read the rest of the reports you'll find that there's no danger of the written material's being damaged."

"I can study the reports on the way out," Lee said. "I must insist, admiral."

"Far be it from me to hold up the efforts of true science," Johns said, with a sigh. He gave orders.

By the time the relatively short trip was completed, Holland Lee felt that he had memorized all the reports sent in by the *Bradley Gore.* He did know by heart every mention of the alien ship and its contents. And he was becoming almost frantic with a suspicion which he could not dislodge.

The fast battle cruiser which had blinked him over eight hundred light-years in only a matter of days rendezvoused with the Exploration and Alien Search Ship *Bradley J. Gore* near a gas giant on the fringe of a solar system. When Lee made the transfer he was greeted by a young officer, obviously a Thumber. She was less than four feet high, and somewhat stockily formed, although she was rather attractive.

Lee had often discussed the known history of the small officer's home planet with his advanced classes. The story of Eban the Hunter and the planet of the small people was not true alien literature, for it had been dredged out of the consciousness of the people of the planet called Tom Thumb, but it was interesting. Lee was in the midst of developing a rather interesting theory that the Thumbers, although their language did not resemble that of the UP, were, like all men, products of one planet, the old Earth. Aside from their size and some abilities to feel radiation, the Thumbers were totally humanoid.

But he had not traveled so far to be reminded of his speculation about Tom Thumb. It was a silly name for a planet, anyhow, and he was surprised that the people there, after a surprisingly good integration into the United Planets system, had not protested the name. They were, however, a people with a certain sense of humor. And their small size and weight made them welcome in the Space Service, where, at times, space was at a premium.

"I am Officer Lani," the small woman said.

He introduced himself, shook her hand and asked immediately when the ship would be going to the ice planet.

"Sir, if you don't mind, I'll let Captain Arlos discuss that with you," Officer Lani said, setting off down a long corridor.

The captain was a man of the old Earth, a Far Seer, his large body in space white, his coned, eyeless head bare.

"You are welcome, Professor Lee," the captain said.

As Lee reached for the Far Seer's hand he felt the ship give a quick and violent lurch. Through an open viewport he saw motion and looked up to see a huge asteroid with a glow of force about it begin to move and then accelerate into the distance.

"You might be interested in our work here," Captain Arlos said.

"Yes, I'm very eager to see the alien ship," Lee said.

"Yes, that, too," Arlos said. "However, professor, I fear that I must detain you for a while. We began our project while we were waiting for you, and it's not something one can stop and start as one might wish."

Lee frowned. The ship lurched again, and another asteroid began to move slowly. He could see small boats working in the asteroid field.

"You should be especially interested to know that what we're doing here was made possible by discoveries made by your illustrious predecessor at the university," Captain Arlos said. "For it was the description of the Bertt drive in the papers translated by Paulus which led to the development of the power system which we're using."

"Captain Arlos," Lee said, "I might be interested if I were not so preoccupied with the possibility of finding other papers as important as the Cygnus Papers."

"I know, I know," Arlos said. "Have patience. I assure you that your precious papers are safe. They have not been touched since we ascertained their nature. They are under guard. The ship has been resealed. They are quite safe and within a few days you'll be examining them."

"A few days?" Lee asked, his disappointment unconcealed.

"Are you familiar with the Bertt principle?" Arlos asked.

"Of course."

"I have to admit that I was one who opposed developing it," Arlos said. He laughed. "I, a Far Seer, saw no need for such enormous power. Space and distance are not overcome by power, but by finesse." He paused. "Have you noted that the power of the small spaceship is very much like a primitive blink generator?"

"Yes," Lee said. "It's curious, isn't it?"

"Quite," Arlos said, as the ship lurched and a huge piece of space rock went accelerating away. "However, anyone who works on a space drive from a foundation of electronics and with a knowledge of gravity will arrive, sooner or later, at the surprisingly simple principle which is the basis of the blink drive. The Bertt drive, that's another matter. It's based on atomics. And it's like going around the block to cross the street. However, we have found a suitable application for it, and I think you're going to see some surprising results."

Lee gave up. He reconciled himself to waiting for several days longer. "Just what are you doing, Captain Arlos?" he asked, as the ship lurched again.

"Take a look," Arlos said, opening a viewpoint and stepping aside as the sixth planet was shown, bloated, huge, impressive even from a vast distance. "There is a term which went out with you Old Ones from Earth," he said. "Until the excavations on Earth, I don't think anyone knew its true meaning. Gas giants of this type, planets with a low-grade nuclear reaction going on in the core, were known as Jovian misses."

"After Jupiter, of the Earth system," Lee said. "A sun that failed to form."

"Exactly. Now consider the most urgent need of mankind."

Far Seers had, on the old Earth, been the sole guardians of knowledge, storing facts in the brains of their genius-moron females, the Keepers. After centuries of being reunited with the other branch of the human race, they still tended to become pedantic now and then. Lee knew the characteristic. "Living room," he said, playing the good student.

"I heard a young Healer express the situation well once, when he thought no one was listening," Arlos said, with that chesty chuckle. "He said, 'The universe don't give a shit, man,' and I tend to agree. The universe *doesn't* care one whit if there are planets suitable for our prolific race to people. As you well know, a lifezone planet is one of the rare and beautiful creations, and they are few."

"I know," Lee said.

"So," said Arlos, "when we find one so nearly habitable as the three planet of this small and insignificant system, we are interested."

"And you're using the Bertt power to toss material into the sixth planet to try to stoke her nuclear fires," Lee said, taking some satisfaction in knowing that he'd deprived the Far Seer of his climax.

"Exactly," Arlos said, unperturbed.

So Lee spent two days watching as the crew of the *Bradley J. Gore* worked to empty a large and expansive asteroid belt of material, using the Bertt power to toss the rocks spiraling outward to finally dive into the atmosphere of the gas giant. It was not uninteresting. The crew of the ship was a typical X&A mixture. The old Earth types were much in evidence, for they took to space readily, loved its freedom and vastness. Healers, those hard-shelled males who could withstand radiation which would kill the Old Ones, or the thin-skinned old form of man, were especially suited to space, for they were born wanderers and could exist quite happily in a vacuum for some time, using stored oxygen from their cells. Power Givers, female, with the ability to soar on the magnetic field of a planet, made hours of instrument measuring unnecessary by simply sensing the almost nonexistent gravity fields around the asteroids and adjusting the Bertt power to total accuracy, to give just enough force to do the job and score a bull's-eye on the sixth planet with each toss. The Old Ones, who were the result of an exodus from the old Earth before the final cataclysm, formed the largest part of the crew, and it was usually an Old One who was in command. Far Seers tended to be more introspective and to avoid positions of public exposure. In this, the jovial Arlos was an exception. He seemed to love all people, and he liked talking. Sometimes Lee wondered, as the days passed, if Arlos didn't speak occasionally just to hear his own voice, for it was Arlos who pointed out the obvious irony of a ship named after the X&A captain who rediscovered the old Earth being the one to find an alien ship.

Arlos ran a tight but friendly ship. Lee availed himself of the opportunity to get to know various spacemen and women, found that he liked the crew's mess better than officer's country, flirted with the little officer who had greeted him, reread all the papers pertaining to the find which awaited his inspection if Arlos ever, ever finished his job of making the sixth planet glow and become a sun.

When the asteroid belt was picked bare, the big ship attacked the moons of the fifth planet. These small and sterile worlds were fed rather quickly to the maw of Six, and it was time for more spectacular feats. The *Bradley Gore*, all generators putting out force to repel radiation, edged into the gravity well of the gas giant and Power Givers measured, Healers worked in the killing radiation to put in place the necessary instruments, and one by one the moons of the sixth planet rode Six's own gravity down, down, to disappear into the planet which seemed to fill the sky.

As a part of the plan, the moons of the sixth planet were used carefully, like billiard balls, to carom against the gas giant at just the proper angle to help slow her rotation. If rotation was not slowed, the rapid spin would merely continue to throw out material by centrifugal force, depleting the planet. And in one spectacularly planned event, the game came to be more like billiards as moon number five was sent rolling toward the planet to crash, on the way, into a rapidly whirling inner moon, slowing it, sending both moons downward.

As the moons neared the planet's atmosphere, great bolts of static lightning hit them, and the show was cheered by all who watched.

"Now comes the ticklish part," Arlos said to his guest, who was a constant companion. The ship blinked on a short-hop and made a thorough examination of the tiny, solid outer planet of the system. When it was positive that there was absolutely no life of any kind there, the Bertt power was put to its greatest test to date and slowly, slowly, the outer planet began to move inward in its orbit. It would be a few months before it added its mass to the mass of the sixth planet.

Since each unit of the system acted and interacted upon and with all other units, the project was more complicated than merely feeding mass to the sun which had failed. Each movement of large amounts of mass had to be carefully calculated. Should the disturbance cause the third planet to leave its orbit, the work would have been done for nothing. Already, small changes had been made in Six's orbital path. And her spin had been reduced slightly, creating some interesting storms in her dense atmosphere. On the third planet, a change in tidal force had caused huge cracks in the ice over the remaining oceans.

Fortunately for the plan, the Titius-Bode rule of planetary distances varied in the system which was being altered. The sixth planet was closer to the sun than was its corresponding planet in the old Earth system, near enough so that even as a dwarf sun she would add heat to the icy world which was the prize. She would be a tiny and insignificant sun, but with her help the ice would slowly melt, the water vapor would be sucked back into the atmosphere. There'd be some peculiar seasons on the planet, for two suns would be determining them rather than just one, but they would be predictable.

From the surface of the ice planet, Six would be about one-third as large as the primary sun. It would be steamy hot on the equator and hot in the summers in the temperate zones. Snow would remain on the icecaps.

Even before the mass of the outer planet was added, Six was cooking internally. Radiation measurements went up daily. She glowed now, in the nighttime sky. Her mass was drawing heavy materials to her core, heating them, shooting out elemental particles. Pressure grew with mass and compacted the core, creating additional heat and stoking the atomic furnace.

Lee had made a friend of a young scientist from Zede II. "Young suns," Lee said to his new friend, "go through extremely luminous stages. They send out such a storm of particles that they sweep the atmosphere from planets. What happens if this one goes that route?"

"Then we'll have to wait for atmosphere to reform before we can use the three planet," the young man from Zede said. "But our calculations show that it won't happen."

"Captain," Lee said, "I'd like to get the artifacts off that planet before your new sun begins to burn."

"I know your concern," Arlos said. "I am assured, however, that we're not going to burn up your planet."

On the way to finish the job, to add the last huge quantity of mass which should, according to calculations, cause the desired effect, Lee studied the icy planet by telescope. It looked quite unimpressive, small, lonely, cold. He tried to imagine what sort of people could have lived there, people who were in space and lived in log cabins.

"Just when?" he kept asking Arlos, but the captain seemed to be preoccupied. He held constant huddles with his staff, with his scientists and engineers, and soon it was decided to put Bertt power on the outer planet and accelerate it. Arlos was not willing to wait out the months it would take for the planet to spin into Six at its current rate. And so the trip to the ice planet was again delayed and Lee witnessed a surge of power which had not been matched, at least not this side of Cygnus, and the planet approached Six at fantastic speed, to be slowed with another massive surge of power.

Six gobbled up a planet. She was that huge, that impressive. And she burped once and glowed. A cheer went up. She was glowing like a moon, however, not like a sun—not with reflected light, of course, but with the weak intensity of a moon to the naked eye. And when Lee learned—Arlos the communicative had neglected to inform him of the true dimensions of the job—that the job still was not finished, he despaired.

"Dammit, Lani," he told his little friend, "Five is a gas giant. I believe in miracles, after what I've seen, but it can't be done."

"With a lever long enough," Lani said.

"I know, I know," Lee said. "But, dammit, how can you apply force to something as nebulous as a gas giant?"

Well, when power is unlimited, you just pour it on, let it

batter every atom, every diffuse wisp of gas, and you move a planet. You move it slowly at first and then faster and you get ready to put on the brakes because you're getting impatient now and you don't want to wait. And if you're an impatient man who wants, more than anything in life, to see a certain assortment of written materials on an ancient spaceship, you drink a lot.

And there *was* Lani. The first time he kissed her he felt as if he were taking advantage of a child. She was so delicate, so tiny.

"I think it could be done best this way," she said, when it became obvious to her that he wanted to kiss her. She stood on a chair.

"I am small, Holland," she whispered later, "but like the small sun we are making, I have a certain glow."

She spoke truth.

And then they watched as two giant planets neared, flowed, atmospheres reaching out toward each other. The radio-band activity was enough so that in a few hundred years it would be detected back on the home planets.

The merging planets formed a solid figure-eight and then, with a rush, became one. The shape was, at first, ovate, then it began to round and with a suddenness which made Holland Lee gasp, a giant flare erupted and streamed upward into the darkness of space.

"Let there be light," Lani whispered, awed.

There was light. Six burned. She seemed to expand. The corona of a true sun grew around her, and her disc bloomed with golden fire as the transformation of hydrogen into helium produced stellar temperatures. Energy flowed out, washed past the ship toward the frozen planet. There would be heat, light, and soon, when the ice began to melt, the settlers would come and there would be life, all the varied life which had once gone outward from old Earth to settle new planets and forget, for a while, its origin.

2

HOLLAND Lee was feeling just a bit under the weather. The celebration party aboard the *Bradley J. Gore* had gone on for hours. And all the while the on-duty crew were moving her at sublight speed back toward the planet without a name, the ice planet. It seemed that he'd been asleep for mere minutes when Lani awoke him with a sweet little kiss and he made a "gawing" sound of protest and sat up.

"Sorry," he said, "things aren't usually so exciting back home."

"You did drink too much," Lani said, with a sly little smile.

"And you matched me drink for drink?" He focused his eyes. She looked completely fresh. "How do you do it?"

"Practice." She smiled. She gave him oxygen and a pill and soon things were looking up. A mess rating served a very good breakfast. Lani was checking her watch. "OK, lover, time to suit up."

A surge of excitement went through him. He followed her into an equipment area and looked for a viewport. When he found one he looked down on a glistening ball, a planet encased in ice. The ship was in close orbit.

Captain Arlos was on the bridge, as usual. "Are you prepared, professor?" he asked.

"I am more than ready," Lee said.

"Since you seem to get on well with Officer Lani," Arlos said—Far Seers did not smile, but there was a hint of amusement in his voice—"I have assigned her to take you down."

"Thank you, sir."